Vicki Blum

The
Shadow
Unicorn

Cover by
Lorne Winters

Illustrated by
David Bordeleau

Scholastic Canada Ltd.

Toronto New York London Auckland Sydney
Mexico City New Delhi Hong Kong

Scholastic Canada Ltd.
175 Hillmount Rd., Markham, Ontario, Canada L6C 1Z7

Scholastic Inc.
555 Broadway, New York, NY 10012, USA

Scholastic Australia Pty Limited
PO Box 579, Gosford, NSW 2250, Australia

Scholastic New Zealand Ltd.
Private Bag 94407, Greenmount, Auckland, New Zealand

Scholastic Ltd.
Villiers House, Clarendon Avenue, Leamington Spa,
Warwickshire CV32 5PR, UK

Edited by Laura Peetoom

Map created by Paul Heersink

Canadian Cataloguing in Publication Data

Blum, Vicki, 1955-
The shadow unicorn

ISBN 0-439-98706-7

I. Title.

PS8553.L86S52 2000   jC813.'54   C00-930822-9
PZ7.B58Sh 2000

5 4 3 2 1   Printed in Canada   0 1 2 3 4/0

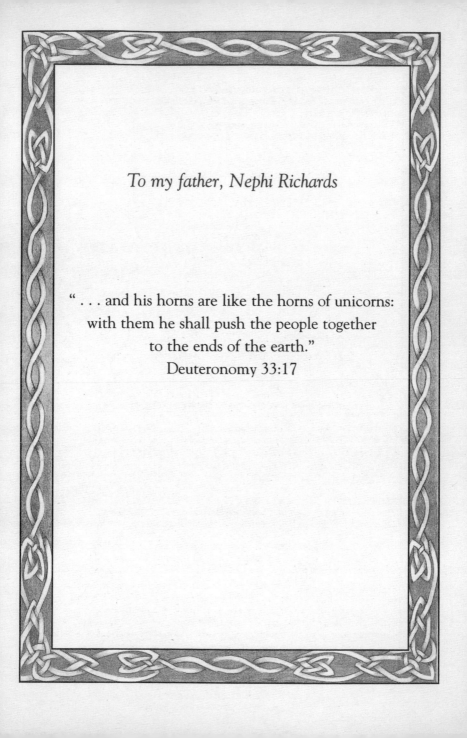

To my father, Nephi Richards

" . . . and his horns are like the horns of unicorns:
with them he shall push the people together
to the ends of the earth."
Deuteronomy 33:17

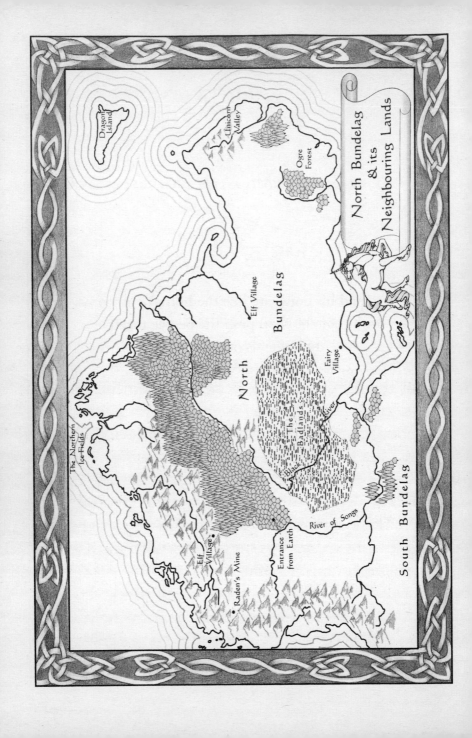

North Bundelag
& its
Neighbouring Lands

Dragon Island

Unicorn Valley

Ogre Forest

Elf Village

North Bundelag

Fairy Village

The Northern Ice Fields

The Black Badlands

River

River of Songs

Elf Village

Raden's Mine

Entrance from Earth

South Bundelag

Chapter 1

For the third time in a week, Arica dreamed about the strange, grey stallion.

She had no idea why she kept dreaming about a horse, especially one she had never seen before. She was beginning to dread the thought of climbing into bed.

In the dream, she stood in an empty corral on a ranch like her cousin Connor's. It was evening, and a huge fire-orange sun was sinking down behind a row of purple mountains to the west. A thin, cold wind whined down off their jagged slopes, plucked at her sweater and tossed dust and hair into her stinging eyes.

As she walked alone across the hoof-marked dirt, she breathed in the thick, sharp scent of animal manure and the sweetness of ripening hay. Above her head an eagle soared, small and black against the red-gold sky.

Halfway across the corral she saw the stallion. He was tied to a post and had clearly been struggling for some time to break free. Clumps of stringy mane were plastered to his damp, grey coat. The air heaved in and out of his lungs as he strained against the rope around his neck. Two small ears lay flat against his tossing head. Wild eyes stared back at her, showing in them more white than colour. The whinny that came from his throat was almost a scream.

Arica approached the horse slowly, murmuring words of comfort. The thrashing eased until she was able to run her fingers gently over his trembling neck. His hide was sweat-soaked and as rough as tangled yarn. There were sores in places, where something had chafed away the skin.

Then she felt his anger and his fear.

Even in her dream she knew this couldn't happen — not with horses, anyway. She pulled back with a gasp, too startled to think. The animal panicked and reared above her, his hooves whipping at air. She stumbled beneath him and fell to her knees. The last thing she saw was two enormous hooves hurtling down upon her . . .

Arica woke, kicking and gasping for breath, nose-down on the floor next to her own bed. Her blankets had followed her and were twisted tightly about her face and neck. As she clawed her way up through the tangle of bedding, her eyes fell upon the little glass unicorn her grandmother had given her for her tenth birthday. It glowed palely, casting faint shadows upon the wall above her head. Through the half-open window a restless wind moaned among the treetops, as if in pain.

Help me, it seemed to say as it whispered through the leaves. *Help him. Help us.*

It was a long time before she slept again.

A few weeks later she met up with Connor after school for a game of soccer. After they had played for a while, some more kids from school came along and joined in. For a time Arica simply enjoyed the frantic racing and the fun. It almost made her forget about the dreams. Almost.

She was just about to score on Connor when she saw the unicorn. It was standing on one side of the soccer net, half hidden by the goalpost. No one else could see it because it wasn't really there. It turned when it saw her looking, and walked away as if it wanted her to follow.

She kicked the ball toward the net, then told Connor she had to leave for a minute. The unicorn was already halfway across the field. The closer she got to it, the more it looked like Wish. But when she finally caught up, it had disappeared.

She stood in the middle of the field, staring around, and waited for it to come back. After a while she gave up and went back to her game.

By the time Arica was done her shower the next morning, she had made up her mind. Out onto her closet floor she tossed binders, books and pencils. From dresser drawer to backpack went jeans, shirts, socks, a toothbrush and whatever else she saw lying around the room that might come in useful. She clattered down the stairs and into the kitchen. Father had just finished his toast. Mother was adding more eggs to a sizzling pan.

The last (and only) time Arica had been to Bundelag, her grandmother had used some kind of magic to make her parents forget she was ever gone. Arica eyed them carefully. Was the magic still in effect? Would it work again? It had better, or she'd never make it past the front door. Her parents, kind and reasonable as they were, would never allow her even one night away if they knew where she was going — let alone a week or more. Her mother and father, she had long ago learned, lived in a very ordered world. They didn't like hitches or bumps, and they insisted on always knowing where she was and what she was up to. Getting to bed on time was their number one rule, never broken. Her life was not at all like Connor's. He could skip into town with his father at ten o'clock on a school night just for ice cream.

All the way through breakfast she wondered what she could say to convince them she had to go. Somehow, Wish needed her — desperately. In the end she settled for the blunt, hard truth.

"The unicorns are in trouble," she said matter-of-factly, rising to her feet. "I'm going to Bundelag. I don't know when I'll be back."

She felt Grandmother's magic, then. It tingled behind her eyes and shivered over her skin like the gentle brush of a dozen tiny hands. She tiptoed toward the door, holding her breath. When she finally arrived without being stopped, she risked one quick glance over her shoulder.

Father had picked up the paper and was frowning at something on the front page. Mother was at the sink swishing out the pan.

"I'm sorry," she said, knowing they couldn't hear her now, lost as they were in Grandmother's spell of forgetting. "But the unicorns need me. You'd understand if you knew."

Then she left quietly, closing the door behind her.

When Arica arrived at Grandmother's house it was just as she had expected — no one answered her knock. Naturally the solution could never be as easy as simply telling Grandmother of the problem and turning it over to her. Life — at least her Bundelag-related life — didn't go that smoothly. Sighing, she fetched the hidden key and let herself in, locking the door securely behind her. The front hall closed in around her like a silent tomb. The little sunlight that made it through the shuttered living room windows cast shadows that seemed to reach and crawl. She moved quickly into the less gloomy kitchen, where the morning sun sprinkled off the pans and the shining tiles. Through the kitchen she went, gritting her teeth as she opened the door leading down to the cellar.

Ten minutes later she was back upstairs again. She had covered every bit of cellar wall with her flashlight, then again by touch, just to make sure. There was no doorway to Bundelag that she could find. Yet, just over a month ago when the trolls had carried her off, there had definitely been something there. A crushing sense of urgency was bringing her close to panic. By now she was sure there was only one thing more dangerous than going to Bundelag, and that was not going. Dangerous, at least, for the unicorns.

She took a deep breath. She would try again. She would try a hundred times if she had to. But as she turned to go back down the cellar stairs it suddenly came to her that perhaps the *how* of going was at least as important as the *where*. Last time she had gone to Bundelag, she had fallen through a crack in Grandmother's floor. Perhaps it hadn't been an accident.

She found the crack easily enough, under a throw rug in front of the dishwasher. It wasn't a very wide crack as cracks go, or very long. No wonder she hadn't noticed it the first time.

Arica held her breath, crossed her fingers behind her back and stepped on the crack.

She tumbled through blackness, while the walls seemed to spin in circles around her head. The fall took longer than she remembered, and the landing felt like it almost loosened half her teeth. She lay quietly for a few moments, trying to figure out if her arms and legs were actually broken or merely battered blue, then concluded that everything still worked well enough. She stood, feeling only slightly dizzy, and imagined making a complaint to Grandmother about the size of that first step. It was a wonder she was still in one piece.

The doorway was easy to find this time. In fact, it stood ajar, as if the last person through had been in too much of a hurry to pull it closed behind.

It was evening in Bundelag, and through the tops of the trees she could see one of the moons just beginning to make itself seen. The other hadn't yet risen. Insects droned. Swallows swooped.

Arica's sense that the unicorns were in trouble was stronger than ever. "Wish?" she called out, tentatively, looking around. Then again, but silently this time, with as much mind-force as she could muster, *Wish?*

No young unicorn bounded out from the trees to greet her. Arica hitched her pack a little higher on her shoulders, took one huge breath to steady herself, and started walking. If the unicorns were in trouble, then the logical place to go was Unicorn Valley. But after just a few steps, she stopped. She had no idea which direction to go. She had never been to Unicorn Valley, and had no idea where it was. She knew she was still very close to the entrance from Earth. But what good would that do her? Any moment now it would blink out of sight, and she'd be hopelessly lost.

She slumped down onto a fallen log and put her chin in her hands. The sad truth was this: she had never travelled in Bundelag without someone to guide her. First there had been the trolls (if you could call being bound, gagged and dragged as "guidance"), then the elf Perye. And of course there were always the unicorns. What use was she to them if here she was, hardly ten minutes arrived, and already needing someone to help her?

Where are you, Wish? she wondered. *Where is Light, and your mother, Song? How can I save you, if I can't even find you?*

The next moment something small and dark and dirty darted out from the trees directly toward her. Arica jumped in panic, screamed and fell backwards over the log into a patch of weeds and thorny shrubs.

This elf was old, short and round like a barrel, with hair the colour of dead grass.

Chapter 2

Arica rolled out from the bushes, pulled herself up onto her hands and knees and gazed into the face of the ugliest creature she had ever seen. He was even uglier than a troll, and that was saying something. There was no doubt in her mind, however, that this was not a troll. What she was actually looking at was a very scruffy elf.

The elves Arica had met in her previous visit to Bundelag were small, slender and golden-haired, with pointed ears that arched elegantly upwards. Even the ones forced to work in the mines had a sort of delicate beauty. But this elf was old, short and round like a barrel, with hair the colour of dead grass. The tips of his large flappy ears just missed clearing the top of his balloon-like head, and he had smears of dirt across his cheeks and chin. His clothing bulged in puckered lumps, dirty and tattered, and his shoes were too large for his feet and pocked with holes. Dangling from his belt was a sheathed sword that dragged in the dirt when he moved.

The elf stepped forward, holding out one grimy hand to Arica. "How do you do, my dear," he exclaimed, bowing graciously. "I'm so pleased to finally meet you!"

Arica stood stiffly without offering her own hand in return. She couldn't help but notice that the top of his head barely reached her chin.

"Who are you? Why are you here?" she demanded, not bothering to keep the suspicion out of her voice.

The elf looked at his hand, frowned, and whipped a dirty rag from his belt. He began scrubbing furiously, talking all the while. "Please accept my most humble service," he babbled, "and may I say what an honour it is to be chosen to accompany you? My nephew Perye has told me about your last great adventure, down to the last detail, and my admiration of you grows with every telling! I will serve you loyally and forever, dear Arica! I wish I could have been there to see you befriend the mighty unicorns and heal Perye's wounds with their magic! Ah, what I would give to have watched you repel the power of the soothstone and destroy Raden's cursed mine with magic fire! And who will ever forget how you crossed the deadly Badlands, survived the clutches of the Black River, and single-handedly fought off Raden — that most evil of fairies — and a hundred of his trolls!" He finished scrubbing his hand at last, and presented it again — looking just as grimy as before — with a flourish. "My name is Nue!"

Arica stared at him in astonishment and wondered how Perye could think this creature was capable of any sense. Perye was a pretty common-sense sort of elf, himself.

"I know what you're thinking," the elf continued, with hardly a pause for breath. "I get it all the time, truly I do. My own dear mother, bless her, named me Nue. I was much newer, then. Ha! Ha! Ha!"

Arica let that one pass without comment. "Did Perye send you, then?" she asked, still with some distrust. The last time she had seen Perye, he and his sister Drusa had been heading home on one of Grandmother's grey stallions. She had no idea where they were now. This bumbling clown might not have been sent by Perye at all. Hmmm — he could even be here for the sole purpose of keeping her from finding the unicorns.

"The Fairy Queen herself bid me come," Nue

stated, puffing out his chest a little and looking her proudly in the eye. "In her great wisdom, she knew you would soon come back to Bundelag, so she sent me to meet you." He pulled a sword from his belt and thrust it into her arms. "She also told me to give you this. It belonged to your father."

"You've got to be joking." Certainly Grandmother could have done better than some old, stubby sword and a chubby, half-witted elf. And where was Grandmother, anyway? Not where she was most needed, that was for sure.

"I would never joke with one as wise and powerful as you, great Arica!"

Arica stared at Nue in surprise. He seemed quite serious. She hated to burst his happy little bubble, but he'd find out the truth sooner or later, anyway. "I'm afraid I'm not as wise or wonderful as you think. At the moment all I am is confused and lost."

The elf looked up at her in disbelief, then his face cleared. "Oh, I understand!" he exclaimed. "You are so kind, so generous. You want me to feel needed. You must know I am here to be your guide, as the Fairy Queen instructed. I will take you to Unicorn Valley to meet with the unicorns."

Arica nodded. Now they were getting somewhere. "That's exactly where I planned to go. There is something wrong with them. I can feel it. We should go as quickly as we can." She took off her pack and stuffed the sheathed sword into it. She would look at it more clearly, later. For now, what mattered was finding Wish, and Light, and Song.

"You can count on me!" Nue whooped, leaping forward.

Before she realized what was happening, he had grabbed one of her hands in both of his. He pressed the back of it to his wide, slobbery mouth. She yanked it free, then wiped it on her jeans as he bent head-down in one final flourish.

"All right," she said, hitching up her pack again. "Lead on."

They hiked for what seemed like half the night. The only good thing about it was that by the time they stopped to sleep she was too tired to care how damp and cold she felt. Nue, clearly having passed this way before, pushed her through a knot of shrubs into a small cave with an opening so narrow she had to slither in on hands and knees, holding her flashlight in one hand and her backpack in the other. She curled up against one wall, trying her hardest not to touch the elf or listen to his non-stop talking, and closed her eyes. It was no wonder he looked so rumpled and unclean all the time if he made a habit of sleeping in holes like this. What she wouldn't do right now for a hot bath and a sink to brush her teeth in.

Her last thought was of hot milk in a mug and fluffy flannel blankets pulled up to her chin.

When Arica woke the next morning the elf was gone. Her initial relief quickly turned into alarm. She would hardly miss Nue's continual chatter and all that nauseating good cheer. On the other hand, she couldn't get anywhere without him.

She crawled out through the hole, dragging her pack behind her.

A small fire flickered cheerfully within a circle of stones. A large leather waterskin lay warming beside the flames. Meat sizzled on sticks. A cluster of freshly picked berries lay neatly upon a large leaf. When Nue saw her he grinned, the smears of dirt on his face dotting his skin like bruises. Morning sunlight sparkled through the leaves above his head, casting tiny shadows that danced and flitted over his tattered coat. He was holding her flashlight firmly in one grubby hand.

"I've learned a bit of magic in my day," he stated proudly, gesturing toward the fire. "Not much, not anything like you fairies can do. Not anything like this wonderful magic light-stick here. But enough to warm our feet by and heat some water for a scrub."

Arica yanked the flashlight out of his hand, turned it off and stuffed it back into her pack. Then she decided that since he'd gone to all the trouble of heat-ing water, she might as well use it.

"I'm only half fairy," she said, splashing water onto her face, "and I have no magic. I only use what the unicorns give me."

"Not true," replied Nue in a know-it-all tone that was beginning to annoy her beyond belief. "It's true you're only a child and your magic is just starting to develop, but you have plenty of magic in you, believe me. All fairies do."

"What makes you the great expert?" she retorted, looking around for something to wipe her face on, then settling for her own shirt.

"I've made a study of fairies and magic."

"That's what Perye used to say."

"Smart lad. Always did take after his uncle."

Arica started to reach for a handful of berries, then giggled in spite of herself. Good heavens, was Nue actually going to use the same wash water that she had? She watched in amusement as he sputtered and splashed, thoroughly drenching the front of his coat. When he was all finished he grabbed a handful of moss and wiped it across his face, leaving behind a fresh smear of dirt.

"Ah, there's nothing like that good clean feeling!" he exclaimed, reaching for some meat. Soon streaks of dark grease ran down his face, mingling with the dirt on his cheeks and chin.

"That explains a lot," she muttered, half to herself.

"Explains what?" Nue mumbled through another mouthful.

Arica figured it was time to change the subject. "You never did tell me what to do with the sword," she said. "Besides drag it everywhere I go, that is."

"That's because I don't know," Nue admitted as he licked juice off his stumpy fingers. "All the Fairy Queen told me was to be sure to give it to you, that it was the right time, and that you would need it. You didn't really expect her to explain herself, did you? Fairies rarely do, you know."

"I've noticed," Arica replied, biting into a chunk of tender meat. "What is this, anyway? It's delicious!"

Nue pointed to the fire, where something similar to a grasshopper, but the size of a sparrow, lay sizzling.

She wished she hadn't asked.

After they were finished eating, Arica helped Nue break camp. She doused the fire with the wash water, then scattered the soggy ashes. The bones, she knew, could be left behind for scavengers. When they were done, she hoisted her pack up onto her shoulders.

"I'm as ready as I'll ever be," she said to Nue.

"Follow me, then," he said, and headed off through the trees.

It wasn't long before they broke out of the forest, and right away she heard the music. At home, rivers trickled, gurgled or roared along their way. But the rivers of Bundelag sang. She could hear one now, in the special way of hearing that happened deep inside, the way that went right to her very heart and bones.

But it was not the River of Songs she heard. That river tingled in her veins like bubbles of sunlight, melting away her pain and fear. No, this was the Black River, with water that sucked life like a leech sucks blood, and darkened joy to hopelessness.

She felt her heart grow sick with fear. Though she had been on her journey only a day, she could see how useless it was. They should turn back now, before it was too late. Plainly the little elf was as stupid as he was ill-mannered and scruffy. What was she doing with such a disgusting creature?

She had to get away! She turned and darted off in the opposite direction, but a firm hand clamped upon her arm, pulling her back.

"Hold on, dear," Nue said. "You'll be yourself in a moment. The rivers always affect your people deeply, for good or ill. The music stimulates the emotion centres of a fairy's brain. At least, that's what the experts say. I've never even heard the music myself, being a mere elf. But it must be true, judging by the way you're carrying on, all hot and angry. It'll pass, sweetie. It'll pass. Just trust old Nue on this one!"

Arica hardly heard him. She lunged forward in an

attempt to pull free, then suddenly found herself face down in the dirt. She gasped painfully while her breath gradually returned. The disgusting little creature had kicked her feet right out from under her. She sat up and glared, trying to spit out words that wouldn't come.

"I had to do something," he said in that annoying, practical way. "To bring you to your senses."

Arica pulled herself up and stomped off, determined not to speak to him for the rest of the day.

It was slow going along the river's dark, winding path, its depressive song dragging on Arica with every step. When at last they left it and climbed into an area of rocky hills, Arica's spirits rose. But not much, and not for long. The sun was hot, bright and naked in the empty sky. A thin breeze rippled the grass on the rocky hilltops and plucked at her hair and clothes. Birds soared, cawing as they climbed. Insects whined and darted. Her pack grew heavier and heavier on her back. And no matter how hard she tried, Arica could not quite shut out Nue's continual chatter.

"Fairies are much too flighty," he rambled as he trudged. "They love to wander, always looking for fun and adventure. Not like my people. We're practical, solid . . . "

She had to admit he was right about that one. Her grandmother would wade into battle, treating it like some grand exploit. Her father had wandered far from his own land, and look where it had got him. He used to be a prince, heir to the fairy throne. Now he was only half-alive, stuck on Earth — a world where he didn't belong — with no memory of the loved ones and the powers he had left behind in Bundelag. A sudden thought struck her.

"Nue, why do I still have my memories?" she asked, forgetting her vow of silence. "I was here in Bundelag, and then went back home. But I didn't forget!"

Nue looked at her like she had just grown two more heads. "Why, you're special, that's why!" he exclaimed. "You're half-human, and tied to both worlds. You have magic all your own, even though you don't realize it yet."

Arica didn't want to think about what this could mean. She didn't want to be special, not as long as it meant having so many hard things to do. But it was a little late to do anything about that now.

They left the hills and struck out over a flat, grassy plain. Evening came, and they simply lay down in the grass and slept. They rose with the birds and went on.

Arica could feel herself beginning to toughen up — or maybe it was just such a relief to be away from the Black River, that all things looked more possible. She could walk more swiftly, and when Nue declared it was time to stop for lunch, she found she had enough energy to appreciate the spot he had picked, a pleasant one with a small spring and a large, flat-topped rock to lean against. It gave them shade and felt cool to the touch. Arica accepted something from Nue that tasted like stale fruit bars, then drank from the spring. She passed on the cheese, however. It had funny little green spots and smelled like the whole cow still in the barn.

When she had finished eating, she simply rested — and it was then that she noticed the silence. It had come upon them gradually, like a series of notes fading into stillness one by one. She stared around at the little clump of bushes, the small rise of ground, the rock they were leaning against. Something ran icy fingers up and down her spine.

"What is it?" Nue asked, grabbing up the remains of their lunch and stuffing it into his bag.

"This is just like the other place," Arica said, staring around uneasily. "And it's too quiet. Haven't you noticed? Where are the birds, the insects, the squirrels? I could have sworn they were here a minute ago." She paused. "Nue, I have a bad feeling about this."

"Get to the point, dear. I'm listening."

"It was . . . It was like this when the trolls and I were attacked by pfipers," Arica continued hoarsely. "You know — the poisonous snakes with wings. Only it's much worse, this time. It's almost like I can feel them fluttering over my skin. Surely Perye told you all about — " She stopped. Nue's skin had gone as white as the buttons on his coat. His body seemed carved of stone. His eyes bulged.

"Please," Arica said, her heart thumping. "Don't say what I think you're going to say."

Nue croaked, "Once you've been bitten by pfipers, you're always more sensitive to their presence."

"That's even worse than what I thought you were going to say!"

"Grab your things and run," the elf howled as he lunged. "Now!"

Their green bodies twisted, glistening in the sunlight.

Chapter 3

Arica's first mistake was to look back. If she hadn't, she might have noticed the mound of dirt that appeared suddenly beneath her feet. As it was, she fell head over heels on top of it, but not before she caught a glimpse of how desperate their situation was. Pfipers filled the sky, bursting in bunches from behind rocks and shrubbery, erupting from holes and cracks in the ground. Their wings rattled like popguns in her ears; their green bodies twisted, glistening in the sunlight. She scrambled forward on all fours until something jerked her back to her feet.

"Head for that patch of prickle bush!" Nue shouted, yanking her arm so hard she nearly fell again.

Arica had no idea what a prickle bush was, but judging by the name, it surely must be some kind of plant with thorns. She'd take a few scratches and pokes over death by pfiper poisoning any day. She moved her legs faster, swatting at the creatures as she went. They were landing now, on her head, shoulders and face, and pounding like hammers against her back and legs.

A few minutes later she realized she would never make it.

Both she and Nue had fallen several times under the assault, and each time it became harder to rise. And they were getting bitten, which meant the poison was slowly building up in their bodies. Arica knew from her last run-in with pfipers that the venom had a delayed effect. Both of them could already be dead, and not even know it.

Then Nue took another tumble, dragging Arica down with him into the grass. The cause of their fall was a deep burrow. Nue started to get up and keep running, then took another look at the hole and plunged his arm inside it, right up to the shoulder.

"Nice try," Arica said between ragged gasps, "but you'll never fit."

Nue drew his shoulder and arm back out. Clutched in his right hand was a wriggling, hissing, furry black-and-white animal.

"Pfipers track prey with their sense of smell!" he shouted.

Arica just stared at him as if he had lost his senses. "This will clean out their nasty little noses!" he explained. Then, howling with glee, he flung the animal into the centre of the pfipers.

"What are you doing!" she shrieked when she saw what animal it was. "That's a skunk you just threw out there! A *skunk!*"

A bitter odour flooded into Arica's nose, down her throat, and sent the tears pouring from her eyes. She buried her face in the mud and grass, but the agony only got worse. Beside her, Nue sniffed and snorted into his sleeve.

"I have no idea what a skunk is," he said, "but the animal I just pulled out of that hole is a stinkrat. There is no more powerful smell in all of Bundelag, and it will drive the pfipers away. You should be thanking me instead of complaining. At least you're alive enough to suffer!"

Arica clenched her jaw, too upset to trust herself to speak. The insufferable little elf was such a know-it-all it made her want to scream. But the next time she dared to look up, it was just as he had said. The pfipers were gone. Thankfully, so was the stinkrat, though it had left behind its mark. Everything within a hundred paces reeked like a sewer.

Nue stood and pulled her up beside him. His face was grey and looked pinched, like his collar was a little too tight. There were purple smudges under his eyes that she hadn't noticed before.

"Nue, I . . . uh . . . I'm sorry," she said, then paused as a sudden spasm of shivering took hold of her body. "I had no right to talk like that. You saved our lives."

"It's all right," he said, patting her back kindly. "That was a close one, much too close. We were both badly frightened." Then, practical as ever, he added, "Come on, let's get going. What we need now is a hot soapy bath."

She nodded and took one deep, shaky breath. "Let's just hope we didn't get so many bites, we *can* keep going."

They got the bath that night, when they came at last to an elf village nestled beside a lake. They weren't actually welcomed in. With averted faces, the elves directed them to a small abandoned hut some distance from their own living area, and conveniently close to the lake. The soap they were given was strong and gritty, and took away everything but the smell.

"Stinkrat odour clings for weeks," Nue explained. "There's not much we can do about that. We'll start out again at first light."

If we can, Arica said to herself, lying down on a narrow wooden cot. If we can . . .

The pfiper poison hit them just after supper.

When the pain started Arica curled up on her cot,

clutching at her stomach. As if through a haze she saw Nue's face hanging somewhere above her, his eyes large with fear. Later she heard his cries of pain rising to match her own.

The last time she had been poisoned, Light, Wish's father, had come and touched her with his healing horn. But she had no idea where Light was, or Wish. All she could think of was that this time it was she who had come to save the unicorns, and here she was lying on a cot, far from Unicorn Valley, doing nothing to save her friends. Some hero she had turned out to be.

The next time she came to her senses, her dead grandfather had arrived.

She noticed him right after she'd been violently ill. When she felt the stomach sickness overtaking her, she had just enough energy to crawl to the door, drag it open, and throw up all over the ground, rather than on the clean floor. She had barely tumbled back into her bed when Grandfather made his presence known by tapping loudly on the nearest wall. She would never have noticed him, otherwise, hovering there just under the ceiling like he was. She stared up at him and groaned.

Grandfather looked down upon her from his mid-air perch, one hand holding a handkerchief to his nose.

"The smell in here would rattle a dragon's teeth,"

he complained in a nasal tone. "What have you done to yourself, child?"

"Pfipers," Arica croaked.

Grandfather nodded. "Hmmm. That explains the bite marks and the sickness, but not the smell."

A long silence followed. Arica's head throbbed; her mouth tasted like she'd been sucking slew water up a straw. "Skunk," she managed to say at last.

"I doubt that," Grandfather said, "since there are no skunks in Bundelag. However, I do believe you've had an encounter with a stinkrat. Unpleasant creatures, those. On such occasions no one wins but the stinkrat. What were you doing so close to one, anyway?"

A pause, then his eyes lit up with understanding. "Brilliant!" he exclaimed. "Of course! Stinkrat smell would drive off pfipers! Nue's clever strategy, no doubt."

Grandfather floated a metre or two nearer to her bed, close enough to pass a gentle hand across her brow. His touch was like feathers and wind. Then he must have forgotten himself and breathed in through his nose, for the next moment he dissolved into a fit of retching and coughing. Arica peered weakly up from beneath her blankets.

"You're awfully sensitive, for a ghost," she whispered feebly.

"I am not . . . technically . . . a ghost," he stated between spasms. His voice seemed to hold a trace of injured pride. "At any rate, my dear," he said, "you're plainly not in the best of health, so I'll be brief. I'll talk, you listen."

Arica nodded. Grandfather had abandoned the handkerchief and gone for his pipe. She had rarely seen him smoke it, only once or twice, but he seemed to receive a great deal of comfort from simply holding it between his teeth.

"My dear granddaughter," he said, in a voice grown quiet and grave. "There is great danger for you here. Your true purpose is now becoming known to the creatures of North Bundelag. Many rejoice, but some would try to stop you, to prevent you from uniting us all in our common goal."

"How can anyone know my true purpose," Arica moaned, "when I don't even know it myself?"

"Hush, child," her grandfather said. "I haven't got much time."

"You never have much time," Arica muttered.

He ignored her and continued, but already his body was starting to disappear. She hated it when he faded out like that, right in the middle of a conversation. It reminded her of someone walking away while they were still talking back at you over their shoulder.

"Be careful, Arica," he said. His voice had grown

thin, and echoed in the silent room. "Watch out for Shadow. He will come . . . " Grandfather paused, then spoke again in a voice like wind moaning through empty caves. "And the sword," he said. "Don't forget your father's sword . . . " And he was gone.

Arica woke to sunlight streaming in through the windows and open door, and the sound of someone chopping wood beneath her window. She rose from the cot, slightly dizzy but completely free of pain. A basin of water sat on a table between the bunks — left there by Nue, no doubt, for his cot was empty. She washed, brushed her teeth and dug fresh clothing from her pack, clothing that smelled only a little less like skunk than what she was presently wearing. She had just done up her last button when Nue stamped on in, his arms loaded with newly chopped firewood.

The elf beamed at her from a face grown pink and cheery with effort, then moved toward the fireplace. "I thought the least I could do was chop some wood for the elves," he explained. "They've been so generous in giving us food and a place to stay."

"You're right," agreed Arica. "We should give them something in return. But we need to get to Unicorn Valley soon, you know."

"True enough. But look at it this way," he replied, grinning back at her. "We survived the pfiper poisoning. How could I be anything but wonderful? I'm still weak, but glad to be alive."

"Did you see my grandfather?" she asked, digging around for her shoes. "He came during the night, and as usual, nothing he said made any sense at all."

"Your grandfather?" said Nue, pausing beside the hearth with his load. "No. Once I stopped retching, I slept right through the night."

"Do you know anything about a shadow, or someone called Shadow?" she said, rising up from behind the cot, a shoe in each hand. "Just as he was leaving, he mentioned something about how Shadow would come . . . " She heard a loud moan and turned to look.

The colour drained from Nue's face like water from a broken jug. He stared back at her. Then the wood slipped from his arms and clattered to the floor around his feet.

Chapter 4

Nue walked away with pursed lips and refused to talk about the thing called Shadow, which made Arica more uneasy than ever. In her opinion, this was the single most annoying thing about the people of North Bundelag. Everybody kept all these secrets from everybody else, and even if they did get around to talking about them, it was always in riddles, which was really the same as not talking at all. Take Grandfather, for example. He was the worst of the lot.

While Nue tidied up the hut, Arica stuffed her belongings back into her pack, along with the food the elves had given them for their journey: dried fruit and meat, biscuits, cheese and, of course, plenty of water. Elves, she had discovered on her first trip to Bundelag, were generous to their friends. (Though they would take a grudge against an enemy to the grave.) She wished she could thank them face to face, instead of with just Nue's chopped wood, but leaving without forcing them to endure the dreadful smell any longer was thanks enough, she decided.

By the time Nue was packed, she was perched on the edge of her cot, ready to go. The elf took one last look around, shoved one or two final objects into his leather bag, and beckoned her to follow.

They trudged up and over low hills the whole day, and by dusk had reached a bare, wind-blown plain with no trees or valleys to protect them. They ate their meal kneeling in the grass. Behind them the sun blazed down in a finale of pink and gold. Insects whined and nipped at their hands and faces. Birds drifted overhead, cawing a last farewell to the dying day.

Just before they settled in for the night, Arica decided it would be a good time to get a better look at her father's sword. She took it out of her pack and drew it from its sheath. It was short for its weight, with a straight double-edged iron blade and a bronze, leather-wrapped handle. It had no jewels or decorations of any kind. It's as unadorned and practical as my father, Arica mused. She gripped it in her right hand and took a practice swing at a passing bat. It darted neatly out of the way and hurried on. The sword hurried on, too, dragging Arica right along with it.

"You might have chopped off a toe," chided Nue, reaching for the weapon. "You need to be careful."

Arica grumbled as she rose, brushing dirt and dead grass from her clothes. "I'd like to see you do better!"

Nue was stronger, so for him the sword was less difficult to hoist. But again, once airborne, the weapon seemed to take on a will of its own. Arica clutched her stomach and howled with laughter as the elf staggered and lurched after the sword, concluding the whole sorry display by tripping over his own feet. "Obviously there's some magic involved here," Nue said as he pried his nose from the dirt.

"Obviously," Arica giggled.

They camped the next night on a high crag overlooking Unicorn Valley. Early the next morning they began the long descent. The closer they got to the valley floor the slower Nue went, until Arica threatened to drag him by his arm.

"It's this place that makes me nervous," the elf admitted. "I've never been this close to unicorns before."

Three hours later they came to an empty meadow surrounded by forest. Leaves rustled around them in a sighing breeze. Ribbons of sunlight pierced through the treetops, sparkling like falls of water as they came. Arica and Nue stepped through the knee-deep grass while birds chirped over their heads and butterflies swirled before their faces in dizzying bursts of white and gold.

Halfway across the clearing they found a statue. It was a beautiful white statue carved in flawless marble, perfect down to every last detail of eyelash and perked ear. It was a perfect likeness of Wish's mother, Song.

Arica walked up to it and placed her hand upon the cool, silken surface of the stone. She ran her fingers gently across it, feeling the ripple of marble hide beneath her skin. And then she knew. No artist could have done such work. Her heart leaped in terror. The breath caught in her throat like swallowed bones. This was no statue: it *was* Song. She pressed her ear to the statue's silent breast. One tiny spark of life still winked faintly, deep inside.

Arica rubbed the statue's nose and inwardly begged for life to return, for breath to begin, for eyelids to blink open to awareness. Only the birds and insects answered, with mournful caws and whines as they dipped and droned in the blue-glass sky. At last she turned away, knowing there was nothing she could do.

She found the next statue a hundred metres away. Song's mate, Light, stood silent and splendid, glittering in the sunlight. A dozen or so other unicorns dotted the clearing, still as the stone they had become.

It was a perfect likeness of Wish's mother, Song.

Nue walked slowly among them, not speaking, not even knowing what to say.

Arica kissed a cold marble face. She pressed her cheek against the gentle arch of a once-powerful neck, and sighed heavily. Bumblebees buzzed in circles above their heads and crawled over the unicorns' ears and sightless eyes. She swatted at them angrily with her hand.

"Wish is all right," she said to Nue. "I can feel it. She's still alive."

"Be thankful for that," Nue replied.

I'm here, Wish, she cried in her thoughts, willing them to travel far. Where are you? Can you hear me?

A sudden breeze parted the branches overhead. Songbirds tittered and dived from restless treetops. Nue whirled, his eyes bright with unvoiced fear. Arica swallowed something hard and sticky in her throat.

"Who did this to them, Nue?" she whispered.

True Arica come! chimed some bells inside her head. The next moment a small white unicorn darted out from the forest, did two laps around her and Nue, bounced over a patch of wild clover, snorted at the bees, kicked her heels in the air and landed, finally, at Arica's side.

Arica flung her arms around the unicorn's neck, only to find herself suddenly flat on her back in the clover patch with Wish standing above her, looking down.

"Stop it, Wish!" she howled, swatting and rolling as the little unicorn nibbled at her neck and ears. "That tickles! Stop it now!"

"I take it this is Wish," said Nue in a stilted, dignified way, looking somewhat relieved but still keeping his distance.

All this awe that elves had for unicorns — awe that bordered on fear — was something Arica never quite got used to. She sat up and pushed Wish away with her hands. "Wish, stop it!" she said again. "I need to know what happened here. Why are the unicorns turned to stone?"

At the mention of the other unicorns, Wish's mood wilted like plucked petals. Large, dark eyes gazed sadly at Arica. Her head drooped.

Bad magic, the little unicorn said.

"So it was a spell, then?" Arica asked. "Who cast it? Why are *you* still all right?"

Gone playing. Came back. Unicorns very sick. Some moved, some didn't. After a while, all stopped.

Arica thought about that. Was the spell like some sort of sickness? "The unicorns all got sick and turned to stone," she explained to Nue. "It may be only a matter of time before Wish catches it, too."

"Catches what?" Nue asked. Then he gasped.

Arica followed the direction of his gaze all the way across the clearing to the trees beyond. Something detached itself from the darkness of the foliage and the overhanging branches, and drifted slowly into view. It froze her where she stood, her mouth open, her eyes wide and staring.

He was the largest unicorn she had ever seen, and he wasn't white like the others. His coat was grey. But not a lovely dapple-grey like the Fairy Queen's stallions, or a soft silver-grey like wisps of cloud against the sunset sky, but a murky, brooding grey. It was the grey of thunder and rain, of angry waves beating on ragged rocks, of swamp mud churning, thick and foul.

And his horn was the colour of clotted blood.

Arica could only stare. She knew where she had seen this creature before. She had sensed there was something unusual about that straining, captive horse in her dreams. But this didn't make sense. She stood and gazed at the unicorn, and slowly her strength was replaced by terror.

The unicorn's eyes locked onto hers, bright with rage. But beneath the anger Arica felt something more, a sense of something haunted and troubled, something reaching out to her. The animal was almost pleading with her for help, like the face of that horse in her nightmare. But then the fire in his eyes went cold, and whatever connection she had felt with the looming grey unicorn snapped like severed twine.

The next moment something bolted toward her,

knocking her feet right out from under her.

Dimly, she felt her body slung over someone's lumpy shoulder. Then they were running, her cheek slapping against his back and her teeth rattling together with every step. It seemed to go on forever. Then she was lying under a hawthorn tree with Wish at her side and something tucked beneath her head. A bedraggled, white-faced Nue was nursing a sickly fire into existence with magic that seemed to be failing him. The shadows from the trees were long and thin, reaching across the ground like arms. Arica gaped at them. How could it be late afternoon already?

She sat and rubbed one sleeve across both eyes, noting that everything seemed slightly out of focus. Her mouth felt like someone had stuffed it with cotton.

"You took the full brunt of the attack," said Nue. "I was worried for a while."

Bad magic, said Wish inside her head.

Arica reached out and stroked the unicorn's silken nose. Wish blew gently into her face. She smelled of roses and sunlight and green grass drenched in dew. Arica opened her mouth to speak.

"No," Nue said, shaking his head. "Don't even ask me what happened. Just rest now and I'll explain when you're more yourself. You're too exhausted right now."

Arica nodded weakly and accepted a cup of steaming soup. She sipped gratefully, her nose nearly dipping in the broth, and wondered where Nue had found all those little potatoes. Not to mention the roots that tasted like onions and carrots, and peas precisely the right colour but shaped all wrong. The elf grinned, as if reading her thoughts.

"There are all kinds of edible plants in the forests of Bundelag," he explained. "You just have to know where to look."

The long silence that followed sent prickles up and down her spine

"I'd like to learn all of that," Arica said slowly. "Will you teach me, some time?" She paused, then added, "If we make it through this alive, that is."

Nue shifted around on the ground, as if he couldn't get comfortable. Then he seemed to decide something within himself, and looked right at her.

Good, she thought, even though the light from their little fire flickered in his eyes like fear. No more hopping around the issue or evading the truth.

"You see," she said, "you don't have to explain it to me now. You forget, I was chosen by the unicorns. They call me their True One. I can sense their thoughts, and they can sense mine. I saw him just before his magic overcame me, so I already know what you're going to say."

"What's that?" said Nue, his voice hardly a whisper.

"You're going to tell me his name is Shadow. You're going to tell me *he's* the one who's changing all the unicorns to stone. No other creature in Bundelag has magic strong enough. You see, I know the truth now. The only one who can do this to the unicorns is another unicorn."

Chapter 5

"He was a good unicorn once," Nue said, "but then things changed."

"What happened to him?" Arica asked, not really wanting to hear, knowing the story couldn't be anything but dreadful.

"Shadow accidentally found his way to Earth."

"My Earth?" Arica asked, staring at the elf in horror.

"What other Earth is there?" Nue asked her. "It is believed Shadow followed someone through the crack — Raden, maybe, or a troll. On Earth he lost his magic, and his horn was invisible to the humans. As a result he was taken for an ordinary horse."

Something like icy fingers closed in over Arica's

heart. "Was he captured — " She stopped, swallowing something that hurt in her throat.

"Yes, he was. While on Earth, he was used for heavy work, and left hungry and in pain much of the time. The man that owned him was not a kind master. Then a few weeks ago Shadow was found, quite by accident."

"Who found him?" asked Arica, knowing the awful answer before Nue even spoke the words.

"Raden. He brought Shadow back and set him free."

"Set him free? *Raden?*"

Nue nodded. "I know — it's hard to believe that Raden would set any unicorn free. Especially since Shadow's power returned to him once he was back in Bundelag. You know that a unicorn's magic is such that not even a fairy dares trifle with it. Well, most fairies, that is." Nue glanced at Arica. She shrugged and looked uncomfortable, so he went on. "There was more to it than that, though. Because he saved Shadow's life, the unicorn was bound to him. Perhaps Raden hoped to use that in some way to win other unicorns to him through Shadow . . . and then somehow take their power."

Arica nodded. "That's the kind of twisted logic he would use, all right."

"So Shadow was free, but he had only been back

with his own kind a matter of days when he attacked another unicorn. He had grown hard and bitter from his treatment on Earth, and so had his magic. He was just too dangerous to have around. The other unicorns had no choice but to act, and quickly. They drove him out."

"Drove him out?"

"Perhaps they should have done more to reason with him," Nue said. "Something to keep him from coming back and taking his anger out on them." He turned away from her, looking sick and shrunken, like the burden of the unicorns' pain had somehow fallen wholly on him.

"How long has Shadow been . . . exiled?" asked Arica at last, absently stroking Wish's mane.

"About two weeks. Well, almost three, now. I heard all this from the Fairy Queen. But I don't think even she knows the extent of the damage that has been done here."

"That's what puzzles me." Arica frowned. "A single attack, even a number of them, I can see, but this . . . He must *hate* the other unicorns, to do this to them."

"He hates everyone."

Fairy and unicorn together, said Wish, leaping to her feet. She bounced over to the hawthorn tree, circled around, then peeked out from behind it at Arica. *Not good.*

Arica laughed and sat up, but too suddenly, it seemed. It took a moment for the explosion of little white lights inside her head to clear away. "Of course we're together, Wish," she said. "And it *is* good."

Wish snorted, bounced around the tree again, and flicked her tail in annoyance.

"Does she actually speak to you?" Nue asked, his voice filled with amazement. "Perye told me, but I find it hard to believe. What did she say? Do you mind me asking?"

Arica shrugged. "She just said something about a fairy and a unicorn being together, meaning her and me, I suppose. She didn't seem too pleased with the idea, though. I wonder why. Sometimes it's hard to — "

Arica stopped, understanding coming all at once, like the upward flick of a switch. Wish wasn't talking about herself and Arica at all.

"Oh, no," she said, staring at Nue, seeing someone else. A fog of horror clouded her brain, and she hardly noticed when Nue's hands gripped her shoulders roughly and shook her.

"What is it?" he hissed in her ear.

"Raden," she said at last, hardly able to force out the words. "Raden and Shadow. *They* did this to the unicorns — together."

Nue covered his face and groaned into his hands.

"If Raden is involved in this," he said, "then — with all due respect — this is more than we can handle. We'll have to go to the Fairy Village and ask for help."

"I think that's a good idea," agreed Arica. "With any luck, Grandmother will be there — or someone might be able to tell us where she is. She'll know what to do. She always knows what to do."

Though it was evening by now, none of them wanted to spend the night in the desolate valley. Wish led them out, much more quickly than they had made their way in, despite the thickening darkness. They spent the next day trekking across the open plains of Bundelag. By nightfall they had arrived at a small river bordering a forest of large, maple-like trees. Winding along the north curve of the riverbank was a row of black-mouthed, rocky caverns. Arica gazed at them eagerly, thinking of the shelter all those lovely caves would give from unwanted wind and rain. Nue shook his head stubbornly.

"This is just the kind of place ogres like," he said, pulling her along. "I think we should keep going for a while. Both moons are up now, so we can see well enough."

Arica groaned her complaint, but Nue won out in the end. They hiked the next while in silence. Beside them, the river gurgled cheerfully, making Arica want to sing and kick her feet in spite of her weariness.

"Can't we just stop for a minute and soak our feet?" she asked the elf.

The next moment Wish burst out from the bushes and landed right between them.

Big things! Big things! her thoughts cried. She circled around them, reared and pawed, then thudded back onto all fours and bounded behind a tree.

"Big things?" said Arica. "What could she possibly mean?"

Nue froze. "Did she say something to you?" he snapped. "What's this about big things?"

But by then it was already too late. A clump of nearby trees seemed to be moving toward them, only a closer look showed her they weren't trees at all. She glanced over her shoulder. Another group was approaching from behind. They were surrounded.

"Ogres," whispered Nue, staring in horror.

Arica had never seen an ogre until this moment, so the part of her mind that wasn't completely terrified found them quite amazing to look at. They were, without doubt, the ugliest creatures she had ever seen. Alongside them, Nue seemed almost pretty in comparison. They were tall — at least two metres in height — and covered with thin brown hair scattered in patches over bare, wrinkled skin. Their ears drooped and their lips bulged. Their teeth were yellow and broken. Above each of their wide, flat noses

"Ogres," whispered Nue, *staring in horror.*

sat one large, oval, green eye.

"Do they have magic?" hissed Arica under her breath.

"They have their own kind of magic," whispered Nue, "a kind any sensible elf avoids like a bitter brew."

"That bad?" she asked.

"Let's get out of here," he said, sounding calmer than he looked. "Do exactly what I do."

"I'm with you," said Arica.

Nue smiled sweetly, nodded politely at the circle of ogres, and took a few steps. The ogres closed in more tightly.

"All right," said Arica. "What now?"

"We'll have to fight our way out," declared Nue. He drew a dagger from beneath his belt.

Arica was beyond being surprised at anything the little elf came up with, but this was just too much, even for him. "One little knife against a dozen monsters two heads taller and twice our weight?" she cried. "What are you thinking! You'll get us all killed, that's what you'll do!" Still, it made her wonder if she should draw her sword, but she'd had no practice with it, really — even if she could get it out of her pack and its sheath before the ogres stopped her.

But Nue was no longer listening. He howled and lunged. Wish bounded out from behind a tree and landed at Arica's side. She could feel the unicorn's power from her half-grown horn, but knew it would never be enough. She gave the command to Wish, anyway. Magic flew from the tip of Wish's horn in sparks of spitting blue.

The ogres pulled back briefly, babbling in confusion. Nue danced before them, shouting and hacking at their knees with his dagger. Perhaps there was some hope for escape, after all. Her hand itched to pull out her father's sword.

Then the creatures rushed forward, stomping and roaring, not touching the unicorn at all, to grab Nue and Arica and pin them to the ground. The battle was over before it had really begun.

Arica learned a lot about ogres as the night went on.

Number One: they weren't mean, just not very bright. When they tied a rope around her waist to lead her along, they seemed almost sorry. And none of them could get the knot right, so it kept coming undone. They bickered about everything, from whose raft was going to carry their captives across the river, to whose mother was going to cook the next meal. Then they kept forgetting, and had to repeat their arguments over and over. To make matters worse, every time they opened their mouths, spit flew in every direction. It made her wonder why they didn't think to swallow saliva once in a while.

Number Two: they spoke only in rhymes. Arica couldn't quite figure out if this was an inherited trait of some sort, or if they had just been taught to talk that way.

Number Three: they had great respect for unicorns. Wish followed Arica closely, yet the ogres didn't try to stop her from doing whatever she wanted. They seemed to have forgiven her for zapping them with magic, and kept peeking at her sideways with their single green eyes. Every once in a while one of them would come out with something like,

"Unicorn holy,
so walk more slowly."
Or,
"Much too chilly
for one-horned filly."
Arica had one of her own to add, something along the lines of:
"If you don't be quiet
I'll cause a riot,
and find a stick
to smack your lip."
But since the main idea was to stay alive and uneaten, she decided it might be best to keep her mouth shut, and see where the ogres were taking them.

After what felt like hours, the ogres stopped in a

part of the forest that seemed to be their home. Then they tied her and Nue to a tree with a guard standing watch over them. All Arica could make out in the darkness was huge, looming shadows moving among the trees. The ogres went about their usual business — whatever that was — without paying her or Nue the slightest bit of attention.

"You're the expert here," said Arica, squinting through the darkness at Nue. "Do they have a weakness, something we can use against them?"

"They don't like sunlight," the elf stated.

"Does it turn them to stone?" Arica asked.

A pause, then, "Whatever gave you that ridiculous idea? Sunlight hurts their eyes, that's all."

"Never mind," said Arica, sighing and wondering where she had picked up that rumour. From home, obviously, where no one knew what they were talking about. Aching with weariness, she crawled as far as the rope would let her, till she found the least lumpy patch of ground. Then she curled up with Wish beside her and closed her eyes.

Nerve-grinding singing woke her some time later.

The first thing she noticed was the campfire. The ogres had built it in a pit beneath the ground, so from where she lay, all she could see were a few flickers of light and some sparks flying upward into the night. It made sense, once she thought about it, for firelight would probably hurt their eyes as well. But the problem was, they needed fire to cook their food. It really was a neat solution. Maybe they weren't quite as dumb as they seemed.

A frame made of tree branches was built above the fire, just high enough so it wouldn't ignite. Hanging from it were pieces of dead animals, roasting over the crackling flames.

Arica stared in horror, wondering if any of the half-raw chunks were elf or troll, then decided she was better off not knowing. Would *she* end up there, tied to a stick, sizzling in her own juices?

"Nue!" she croaked to the sleeping lump beside her. "Are they going to eat us next?"

Nue groaned and rolled over. He sat and blinked a few times, his face shadowy and haggard in the flickering light.

"I'm not sure," he said, rubbing at his eyes. "I haven't heard of any actual cases. But there have been elves that disappeared into ogre country, never to return."

"Thanks for making me feel so much better," she said.

The ogres' singing rose in a shivering, whining crescendo. Some of the ogre children danced in flat-footed, clumsy hops. An ogre version of ring-around-the-rosie seemed to be taking place. A few of the females had spread grass mats out on the ground. Several clay bowls were being placed alongside each mat.

"This must be their way of setting a table," Arica said, half to herself.

A group of ragged males burst from the forest and circled the fire pit. Their harsh laughter rattled in the night like old motors.

Arica reached out and rubbed Wish's neck, then pressed her cheek against the animal's silky mane. "If they start to cook us, I want you to get out of here," she said to the unicorn.

Won't cook, said Wish. *Just don't trust. Don't know what to do with you.*

"Well they seem to trust you!" she exclaimed. "Is there anything you can do to help us?" But before Wish had the chance to reply, sheer bedlam broke loose among the ogres. They suddenly started milling about in a swirl of confusion, stumbling over and into one another, all shouting at once.

"Help quick,
she's sick!" cried one.

"Ate a bone
Leave alone!" wailed another.

"What on Earth is going on?" asked Arica, forgetting that at the moment she was as far away from Earth as she could get.

The ogres hopped and howled. One of the children had slumped to the ground and lay without moving. One that looked like a mother shrieked above her.

"I think that little female is choking," said Nue.

Arica jumped to her feet and yanked on the rope around her waist. It held fast — for a change. It was probably the only good knot the ogres had tied all year. She turned to Nue. "Do you have another knife hidden on you somewhere?" she demanded.

"If I did, don't you think I'd have freed us by now?" he snapped back.

"Thilug choke!

My heart is broke!" cried the mother, flapping her canoe-paddle hands in the air.

Even in the semi-darkness Arica could see the tears pouring from her one green eye, running down the lines in her ugly face. "Nue, we can't just do nothing!"

A large male ogre was pounding his chest, his face raised to the sky. Arica flinched with every blow. It was amazing he hadn't driven his ribs through his lungs.

"Much too late!

What bad fate!" he bellowed.

Arica flung herself against the rope. "Wish!" she cried. "Help me, Wish!" Wish bounced up to Arica, whinnied, nuzzled her shoulder, then touched the tip of her horn against the rope. It unravelled and fell free.

"Now why didn't you think of that sooner?" asked Nue. "We could have been out of here hours ago!"

"Thank you, Wish," Arica said, and ran.

The ogres were in such an uproar that they hardly noticed her until she was right there among them. Thank goodness the victim was a child, or Arica would never have been able to lift her. Grabbing the child from behind, she heaved her up, hoping with all her might that ogres' stomachs were in the same place as humans'. She put the heels of her hands in the centre of the girl's upper abdomen, and pulled in and up with one big thrust. Nothing happened. The ogres shrieked louder and moved in. She tried again. Still nothing.

Again. Nothing.

Again.

A slimy, reddish piece of bone flew out of Thilug's throat and up, hitting the ogre mother right above her eye with a resounding *thunk*. The circle of ogres stood and stared stupidly at Arica. Then the mother shrieked with joy and clutched her gasping daughter to her breast.

Chapter 6

Morning had come. Above Arica's head the trees caught dawnlight in their branches and scattered it like showers. It flickered in patterns of green and gold across the forest floor. She breathed in the scent of forest moss and flowers, of dew and leaves and rotting logs, and felt glad to be alive.

The ogres, for the most part, had returned to their caves for the day. Only Thilug and her parents remained behind, to bid Arica, Nue and Wish good-bye. The ogre family stood together, blinking in what to them was quite a glare. Thilug grinned, looking much like an ordinary little girl with thick arms and one eye too few. For some reason her teeth had managed to stay white and reasonably straight. They won't be for long if she keeps gnawing on all those bones, mused Arica.

Thilug's father stepped forward with something in his hand. Arica took the small package he offered and started to unwrap it, but the ogre shook his head.

"With ogre sight,
no need to fight.
Remember its power
for darkest hour."

Arica stared up at him, trying to make sense of the rhyme.

Nue moved closer. "He's giving you what, in his opinion, is the greatest thing an ogre can give," the elf quietly explained. "It's an ogre eye, taken from one of his dead relatives. Eyes are very sacred to ogres."

Arica shuddered and tried to keep the smile fixed on her face.

"It is said ogre eyes hold great magic," Nue continued, "but it's a wild magic, and quite dangerous. They say it will show you marvellous visions, and even, on occasion, reveal the future. The problem is, no one has ever looked into an ogre eye and stayed sane enough to tell the tale." He dropped his voice even further. "I'd toss it into the first puddle I came to, if I were you."

Thilug's mother explained:

"This is our gift,
for your journey swift.
May your travels hereafter
be filled with laughter."

Arica thought for a moment, then slipped the package into her pocket. "They don't mean us any harm," she said to Nue. "I'll keep it."

"By the way," Arica said to Nue later as they walked across yet another vast plain, after they had left the ogre's forest behind them. "What were the ogres cooking last night?"

"I didn't dare look too closely," the elf admitted, "and I certainly wasn't about to ask. But I don't think there were any elves hanging over that fire, or trolls, either. Definitely no humans, if that's what you're worried about."

"I don't think they would have eaten us, then," Arica said, glancing sideways at Nue. "Do you?" The elf remained silent. "Nue?"

Wish bounded up suddenly on the other side of her. "And what do you have to say?" she said, turning toward her. "What do you think ogres eat?"

Many things, said Wish's voice inside her head. *But not the same kind of food as fairies or unicorns.*

Arica jumped in surprise, then grabbed Nue's arm. "She did it again!" she exclaimed, pounding on his shoulder. "Isn't it wonderful! She spoke a complete sentence!"

"It makes no difference to me," said the elf glumly, "since I can't hear her, sentences or not."

Arica glanced over at him. She wondered what had made him change from the cheerful, gallant fellow of these past few days to the sour, worried elf he was now.

That night, camped on the prairie, she found out.

After their usual forage-the-surroundings meal, spiced up with berry cakes and wild goat milk provided by the ogres, the story at last came out.

"During the night," Nue explained, "after you fell asleep, the ogre that was guarding us started to talk. I thought, why not listen, maybe I can learn something, or at best win his sympathy. He was hard to understand at first, but after a while I got the hang of it.

"He told me there were rumours all through the forest, rumours of elves once again working in Raden's mine."

"It can't be true!" protested Arica. "The Fairy Queen would never allow it."

"Yes, that's true," said Nue. "She forbade Raden to make elves work against their will. But what if they *choose* to work in his mine?"

"They never would," she said with certainty. "You forget, I know those elves. I worked beside them in that mine. I fought with them for freedom. They would *never* work for Raden."

Nue rubbed fingers across bristly brows. "Well, there's a rumour going around about a valuable discovery in the mine. It could be silver they've found, or even gold. The ogre told me the elves are working again, but they are no longer held by ropes. You're right about one thing, though. Most of the elves, like Perye and Drusa, will stay as far away as they can from Raden." He paused. The breath left his lungs in a painful hiss. "But others might not. Especially if they are tempted by riches."

"No longer held by ropes? Tempted by riches? I don't believe a word of it," said Arica. "And I don't want you to believe it, either. It's a rumour, that's all. It must be!"

Then she grabbed her blanket, rolled up inside it, and tried to sleep.

By mid-morning of the second day after they'd left the ogre's forest, they arrived at the road leading into the fairy village.

Nue stood for a moment looking longingly down it, then sat with his back against a rock and sighed. "I'll be here when you get back," he said, plucking up a twig and poking at his teeth.

Arica stared at him in dismay, then at the road that, as far as she could see, led to nowhere. It was made of flat rocks fitted together. It wound its way from the grassy field they were standing in, across a small bridge built over a stream, then down a gentle slope to the seaside beyond. There it ended, smack in the centre of a sandy beach.

"Only one problem," Arica said, throwing her pack on the ground and plopping down beside it. "There's no village."

Wish leaped over her pack, circled once, then bounded with clacking hooves across the road.

"Ah, but there is," Nue insisted. "You just can't see it."

Arica thought it over for a moment. "I see. They've covered it with magic."

Nue nodded. "It wasn't that way before. It used to be that there was nothing hidden in Bundelag. Now you couldn't find your own teeth if you set them beside your dish."

Arica giggled at the thought of Nue trying to chew with bare, shrunken gums. "Then you're not coming?" she asked.

"Since the Great War, only fairies are allowed inside the fairy village."

"What about Wish?"

"Unicorns go where they please," said Nue, shutting his eyes.

It was plain to see he was finished explaining. Arica took up her pack and headed down the road with Wish's hooves tapping out a tune on the stones beside her. Over the bridge she walked, to the end of the road, to the stretch of golden shore and the hazy blue sea lapping cheerfully up against it. She stopped then, looking back, and shrugged at Nue as if to say, what now?

Nue was gone. So was the field, the bridge, and even the road.

It seemed to Arica that the sun had burst down upon her in great glory, scattering light like blowing leaves about her head. She stood and blinked, trying to make sense of the dazzling display before her.

The fairy village was magic made beautiful. Many-coloured cottages sat amid shrubs and rows of flowers. Springs of water burst from beneath boulders and gurgled through gardens and hedges. The cottages were arranged in tidy clusters, with walkways running in between. Behind her, a dazzle of azure ocean melted into the sky.

As Arica paused at each doorway, knocking and listening, she realized at last that the fairy village held no fairies. She and the unicorn travelled the streets alone, calling to empty doors.

Gone, said Wish, nuzzling her hand.

"Yes, but where?" she wondered aloud.

Finally, because she could think of nothing else to do, she made her way toward the castle that loomed

She made her way toward the castle that loomed tall above the cottages.

tall above the cottages. Wish moved quietly beside her. As she hesitated before the massive turrets and stone walls, the drawbridge glided slowly downward like the settling of some great, silent bird.

A man walked forward to greet her.

Her first impression was of kindling loosely tied, or of driftwood, so light and dry it felt almost hollow. The man looked like he was made of paper stretched over bones, but when his gaze rested upon her she saw magic in his eyes.

"True One," he said as his hand brushed her own. "Greetings. I am Doron, the Keeper of the village. It is my job to watch over it, and keep it as beautiful as it is now."

"I'm pleased to meet you," she replied.

He bowed his head to Wish. "A unicorn is always welcome here."

Arica didn't see much use in wasting any more time on pleasantries when there was so much she had to know.

"We've come a long way," she said in a rush of impatience. "Do you know where my Grandmother is — the Fairy Queen? And where have all the fairies gone?"

A look crossed his face like he'd just caught a glimpse of something better left unseen. He cleared his throat and rubbed at his brow with a hand of knuckles and bones.

"Your grandmother is at the border of the land, where fighting has broken out." He paused, as if the words had somehow left a wound.

"And the other fairies?" Arica asked.

"Others?"

The way he said it made Arica's heart plunge. She stared back at him, hardly breathing, waiting for words she didn't want to hear.

"Yes," he said at last. "You know the terrible secret, now. There are no other fairies. There is only myself, the Fairy Queen, and the Queen's son Raden. And now you, my dear Arica. All the others were lost on Earth when they went to close the cracks between the worlds."

Chapter 7

The thing that impressed Arica most about the Fairy Queen's castle was the table in the great front hall. It reached up from the cold stone floor like a giant's fist, gnarled and ancient, with fingers that twined and twisted as they spread. The top of it was carved of polished ebony, smooth as glass, and inlaid with a glitter of rainbow gems.

And the magic! It glistened in the air like silver dust; it settled into cracks in corners and under doors; it fluttered like plume moths against her skin.

Arica sat at the table while Wish waited nearby, nibbling on the apples and oats Doron brought in for her on a wooden plate. He gave Arica grapes and cheese, chunks of warm wheat bread dipped in butter and honey, and apricot nectar so cold it hurt her throat.

When they were done eating, she brushed her fingers across the smooth-worn wood, and felt them tingle with a deep and ancient magic. Doron peered at her from under bushy white brows.

"Look," he said. "Something is happening."

Swirls of light and darkness whirled across the tabletop. Bubbles of air and sunlight swelled and broke, to scatter rainbows in their wake. Then a picture slowly formed in the centre of the spiral, and out from the fractured images looked her own grandmother, the Fairy Queen of Bundelag.

Grandmother was mounted upon one of her great grey stallions, while a battle raged around her. The elves at her side marched forward in rows, struck against the human soldiers and their guns, then fell back in terror and confusion. Arica watched as long as she could bear to, then turned her face toward the wall.

"Look again," said Doron gently.

She was hardly able to do it. But this time, only Grandmother remained, already fading from view. Arica gazed at her, and the Fairy Queen's eyes met hers across the distance that separated them. Then, just as the twist of colours scattered her away, Grandmother spoke out two single sharp words: "Stop him."

Arica sat for a long moment, staring at nothing, then raised her eyes to Doron.

"Does Grandmother use this table often?"

Amusement gleamed in the old fairy's eyes. "For eating — yes. But until now, the magic has not shown itself. Perhaps it was just waiting for the right person. I do believe great things are about to happen because of you, young Arica."

Arica nodded, hardly hearing his words. She walked over and placed her hand on Wish's neck. The unicorn nuzzled at her fingers.

"I'm sorry, Keeper," she said to the old man, "but we have to go. Grandmother has made it clear what I have to do." She shivered. "I hoped I would never have to see Raden again."

"With family, that isn't always possible," he said, sounding sorry. "Good-bye, dear child." His voice was like dry leaves blowing over old bones.

He walked with them to the front gate and stood watching, looking old and alone. The castle of crystal and gold glittered under the high noon sun as the drawbridge closed behind them, shutting him inside.

Arica followed the stone road back the way she had come. There she found Nue, still sleeping under a tree. She curled up nearby with Wish at her side, and soon joined the elf in slumber.

When they woke a while later, Arica told Nue everything that had happened inside the fairy village. He seemed especially interested in the table and its magic, and made her go over the story several times.

"Forget the table," she said at last. "Right now we need to find Raden."

"The mine is here," Nue said, drawing a sketch of Bundelag in the dirt with his finger. "If we go this way," he continued, making a downward curve, "we'll avoid the Badlands. But we'll have to ford the south end of the Black River. That will be unpleasant, to say the least, but less dangerous than actually going through the Badlands. However . . . " He paused and frowned. "Going through the Badlands would be shorter, and crossing the shallow north end of the river much easier. Did you get the feeling the Fairy Queen wanted us to hurry?"

Arica looked thoughtfully at his drawing. "Grandmother seemed more worried about how the battle was going than anything else. But let's see . . . " She ticked off the items on her fingers. "The elves might be losing their lives. The unicorns are turned to stone. Raden is paired up with the most powerful animal in Bundelag. Yes, I would say we should take the shortest way, in spite of the risks."

"I was afraid you'd say that," said Nue. "I've never

travelled through the middle of the Badlands, you know. But it couldn't be much worse than the time a friend and I set sail for Dragon Island. Some would say we were out to slay dragons, but take old Nue's word for it — our reason was more noble than chasing after creatures that probably don't exist. Unfortunately, after two days a violent storm overtook us. The waves were so high they nearly — "

"That's a wonderful story, Nue," Arica interrupted, "but now is not the time. We have to get going. When it comes to the Badlands, no amount of experience will help, trust me. Are you ready?"

Nue shrugged. He slung his bag over his shoulder and tightened his belt. "As ready as I'll ever be," he said, and turned them reluctantly to the west, and Raden's mine.

They arrived at the border of the Badlands the next day. Arica stood for one long moment and stared out across the black horizon, remembering. Off in the distance, soot billowed up in great clouds. Nearby, the sky hung clear and blue, changing gradually until it sickened to a greyish haze above the jagged hills. Here where they stood, insects darted and birds soared, catching wind and sunlight in their wings. There, nothing moved but the dust, gritty and thick with heat. She remembered the Black River screaming in her head as it tumbled through the broken rocks below, and shivered, turning away.

Bad river, came Wish's thoughts.

"You haven't forgotten, either," Arica said, turning to the unicorn and fondling her ears. "My goodness, you're growing! I've never had to reach this high before!"

Growing, said Wish.

"Standing here and staring at it won't make it go away," said Nue. "Let's get this over with." And he headed off through the soot. Arica sighed, hoisted her pack higher on her shoulders, and followed.

For the first few hours, things went better than she expected. It was true that the dust blackened their feet and clothes, clogged up their noses and mouths, and seeped into every crack and wrinkle of skin. But at least nothing was trying to eat them, and the later it got, the cooler the air became. By evening the temperature was almost bearable.

"Have you ever spent a night in the Badlands?" asked Nue, leaning against a leafless, twisted tree and wiping his sooty face with an even sootier sleeve.

Arica shivered. "I'd rather walk all night," she said. "The sooner I'm out of here, the better. How do you feel about it, Wish?"

Keep walking, agreed Wish.

After a brief meal that left them half-hungry and

unsatisfied, they continued their dismal trek.

Sometime after sundown, the wolf arrived.

Nue saw it first. He stopped in his tracks so suddenly that Arica nearly tripped over him. It stood off to the right of them, so far away that for a moment she thought it was just a thicker swirl of dust thrown up by the rising wind. It melted away, then reappeared a little closer.

It was the biggest, blackest wolf Arica had ever seen, and it had red eyes. They glowed through the thickening darkness like two tiny fires, and they were fixed unblinkingly upon her.

"Wish," Arica whispered desperately to the unicorn, "I sure hope that's one of your wolf friends out there, because if it's not, we're in a whole lot of trouble."

I do not know him, said Wish.

"What did she say?" hissed Nue to Arica.

"Nothing you want to hear."

It wasn't long before Arica realized the wolf was not their only problem. The wind was rapidly turning to a gale, a gale that whipped dust and grit in circles about their heads and tore branches off the nearby trees. The wolf howled, almost upon them now. They stumbled through the growing tumult, heads down and their backs hunched against the blast. In the dimness ahead, two eyes burned, hot and bright as lamps. Then the wolf leaped directly into their path.

The wolf howled, almost upon them now.

Chapter 8

They swerved to avoid the wolf, almost falling over one another. Nue yanked on Arica's arm just as the streak of fur and teeth shot past. The animal turned and galloped beside them, so close they could feel the heat from its massive body.

After a while Arica realized the wolf was forcing them to go in a particular direction. A while later all she cared about was staying on her feet and ahead of the snapping jaws. Oddly enough, she sensed no fear of it in Wish, only a concern that they wouldn't make it in time.

She wondered where it was they were supposed to be going.

It wasn't until she stumbled through a large cave opening and sank weakly onto a rock-strewn floor that she realized what the wolf had done. As she lay, curled up and panting for breath in a dark corner while the storm shrieked on past, she knew they could not have survived much longer outside. The wolf had saved their lives.

Nue grinned down at her, his face lit by the flashlight from her pack that he now clutched lovingly in his hand.

Safe, now, Wish said, blowing warm air into Arica's face.

The dense black shape of the wolf stretched soundlessly across the cave's entrance, radiating heat and the scent of dirt dens in hillsides, of animals newly killed, of nights spent running beneath full moons. She couldn't help but wonder if the wolf was trying to keep the danger out, or keep them in. For now, it amounted to the same thing. They weren't going anywhere and neither was it. She slept.

When she woke, it was almost morning. The storm had blown itself away, and the wolf was gone.

As Arica crawled stiffly out of her corner and stumbled toward the doorway of the cave for a look outside, she saw in the dim light a pile of strange dark objects, shaped somewhat like footballs.

Nue followed her over, lifting one up with his

hands. "They're underground gourds," he said, brushing away the soot that covered it. "The wolf must have dug them up for us." He shook his head in amazement. "That was the smartest wolf I've ever encountered." He paused, then added, "Actually, it's the *only* wolf I've ever encountered."

"I don't know how or why it turned up like it did," Arica mused, "but I think it had something to do with Wish. Wolves seem to like her a lot. One time she brought a whole bunch of them to help free me from Raden."

"I'm glad I wasn't there," admitted Nue. "It must have been quite a sight."

Arica nodded. "It was. Even the trolls were scared."

The next moment Wish bumped into Arica from behind, almost knocking her over. When the unicorn saw the gourds, she bounced over the pile, flicked her tail in the air, whirled around and began knocking on one of them with her hoof. After a few blows, one end broke open. Wish lapped up the fluid that poured out, whinnying with obvious pleasure. It didn't take Arica and Nue long to follow her example — they drank all they could, then ate the flesh. Before they set out again they stuffed as many as they could into their packs.

When they finally stumbled out of the Badlands late that afternoon, the gourds were all used up. They found a spring trickling out through some stones and drank thirstily. Then Nue filled the waterskins. Arica gazed around, glad to be back where the trees actually had leaves and the grass grew lush and green.

By the time they arrived at the Black River just hours later, dusk had fallen. They crossed the river at its most shallow part. It took all of the willpower Arica possessed to wade even knee-deep through the sluggish, sludgy mess without screaming right out loud. The mud on the bottom dragged at her feet as if it meant to suck her down, but that wasn't the worst of it. What she hated most was the sound the water made: it swelled like screams of pain, then grew quiet as a hiss, then swelled again. She gritted her teeth and looked enviously at her companions, who splashed cheerfully on, hearing nothing.

At last they clambered up the bank on the other side. Arica insisted that they get a good distance from the river before they set up camp for the night. The last thing she needed was for it to keep her awake.

She was relieved when they all slept well, and that the forest was visible when they woke the next morning. That meant — if Nue was right — that they were only a few days' journey from Raden's mine.

"At least we don't have to worry about a surprise attack from ogres," Nue stated cheerfully as they trudged through the forest.

Arica laughed. "You're right about that. Now all

we have to avoid are the bears, trolls, pfipers and whatever else is lurking in here!"

Around noon, they stopped at a small stream to drink. While Nue filled the waterskins, Arica went foraging. By this time she was starting to recognize many of the edible plants that grew in North Bundelag. She came back with an armful of spinach-like leaves, some mushrooms and a few chunks of bland but edible bark. Then they went on, making such good time that by mid-afternoon she could see that they were reaching the far edge of the forest. The trees had grown thin, letting through sunlight that sparkled on the leaves and flickered off the forest floor. Nue darted off the path and came back a short while later, grinning as he offered a handful of berries. "They're called crownberries," he said, revealing his purple-stained tongue and teeth. "They're my personal favourite. There's nothing like a piece of crownberry pie, fresh from the oven . . . " He seemed lost in some distant, delicious memory.

Arica took some and chewed. "Hey, these are saskatoons!" she said, reaching for more.

"I don't know what saskatoons are, but these are crownberries," Nue insisted. "See how the top of the berry is shaped like a little crown?"

"Well, that may be so," said Arica, "but these berries are definitely saskatoons."

"No, they are not — " began Nue, but that was as far as the argument got.

Arica looked at him, then followed his gaze to see what he was staring at. A dozen trolls or more were striding toward them, with knives pulled and swords drawn. The group paused some distance away. One troll continued forward until he stood before her.

His tattered blue jacket was even dirtier than she remembered. His pants hung loose, like rags off bones, and were too short for his legs. A ragged shirt-tail that was crusted with old food spilled from beneath a belt of twine. The hate in his eyes could have lighted a room.

"Od," she said, swallowing fear. She could feel his eyes upon her face like spots of liquid flame, but decided to brave it out. "How have you been?"

"I've never been better," he sneered through his black, broken teeth. "It's business as usual for us. Seems your little temper tantrum did us more good than harm. After you blew up the mine, there was some clean-up to do, but things are better than ever now."

"I'm so glad to hear it," she said.

"I bet you are," he replied in a voice like grinding gravel.

Wish stepped in closer. The troll cleared his throat. His gaze slithered scornfully over the animal.

"A live unicorn," he growled. "That's a problem soon to be fixed."

"What do you mean by that?" demanded Nue, jumping forward. Arica tensed, wondering again if she should draw her sword, but deciding against it. They could not possibly win, and Od would only take it away from her. Hopefully Nue had the sense not to yank out his dagger when they were so hopelessly out-numbered.

"You'll see soon enough," said Od, showing them his first real smile. "Come with us, if you don't mind. You're our guests. Raden is expecting you."

Chapter 9

A miserable two days of walking brought them within sight of the mine. On Arica's earlier visit, the mine had been protected by a spell to keep it hidden and isolated. This time, when they crested the last hill, they could see a small huddle of buildings spread out below them, deep in the shadow of the black, broken mountain.

Arica could hardly believe Raden's boldness. Was he so sure of himself that he no longer feared anyone or anything? She shivered, but not with cold.

Wish stood beside her, breathing warm air onto her cheek. *True Arica will save the unicorns,* she said.

"I wish I believed in me as much as you do," Arica replied grimly.

The trolls led them through the gate into the compound. They had done some rebuilding in the time since the battle and the fire, but they still had a long way to go. Scraps of old wood had been used to make what few repairs were completed. Some buildings had not been touched. Doors hung on hinges; broken windows abounded; holes left rooftops open to the sky.

Arica caught Od's eye and almost said something, then choked back the words. If she pointed out that things weren't as wonderful as he'd let on, it would only make him angrier. She was here to save the unicorns, not bicker with the trolls. Better not to lose sight of her goal now, not when she had come this far.

Then a door opened and Raden was walking toward them, tall and dark-haired, heart-lurchingly like her father — in appearance, at least. Arica's stomach rolled; she felt her fingers tighten into fists. Easy, she told herself. You can do this. He only tried to hurt you a few times. He only tortured the unicorns for a little while. Perhaps it's not his fault they're all back in Unicorn Valley, turned to stone. Perhaps this is all a terrible mistake.

Raden paused, watching them and waiting. Od led their little group closer and stopped, smiling smugly to himself. Arica and her uncle regarded each other from across the space between them. Tension thickened the air like smoke.

"My dear niece," Raden said, his voice smooth and neutral. "I'm so pleased to see you again."

Too smooth and too neutral, Arica decided. "Uncle," she replied, deciding to play the same genteel game, "I'd like you to meet my friend, Nue. And Wish, of course, you already know."

"Pleased to meet you," said Nue, bowing in grand elf fashion.

"My pleasure," said Raden, nodding. Then he turned to Wish. "Ah — a unicorn!" he exclaimed. "Not many of those left in Bundelag, I've been told." He shook his head in mock dismay. "Too bad, too bad, but these things happen. This is such a . . . a rare treat to have you drop in like this. What brought you all the way out here, may I ask?"

His eyes flicked back to Arica, gloating black eyes, full of spite and loathing, and she knew the battle between the two of them had begun. Or, to put it more accurately, the battle that had begun months ago had started anew.

"How nice of you to send out a welcoming party," she replied coolly.

"My pleasure," Raden said with a sneer, and turned to Od. "Escort our guests to their rooms. When they

. . . tall and dark-haired, heart-lurchingly like her father . . .

have rested and refreshed themselves, have my niece join me for a late dinner." Then he nodded good-bye, leaving them to be taken care of by the trolls.

She had no complaints about the quarters they were given. Od took them to a small shed with an overhanging roof on one side. Someone had covered the ground beneath it with hay, filled an oat bucket, and set out clean drinking water. Inside, the two rooms had beds, blankets, soap and water, and towels.

"It sure beats the pit," said Arica to Nue as she gazed around. "That's where he put me the last time I was here."

"It looks inviting, but don't let your guard down," advised Nue.

When Od came for her later, she was ready. She hugged Nue good-bye and followed the troll outside. At the doorway to Raden's home she paused, breathed deeply, and stepped inside.

Nothing much had changed as far as she could tell. The heads and bodies of stuffed animals still adorned the walls and floors. Some new trophies had been added, some old ones taken away. She entered without speaking and sat on the edge of her chair. They ate and drank in silence. She didn't touch her meat.

Then something pulled at her through the open window. The call, whatever it was, went straight to her heart, like a whisper of pain borne on a summer wind. Raden offered her pudding and cream, which she declined. They sat looking at one another across the snarling face of a polar bear rug. Her stomach had taken on a life of its own. Shadow, it must be him . . .

"Was it my cooking?" asked Raden, smiling with amusement. "Your face has turned a rather gruesome shade of green."

"You know what it is," she said, sweat breaking out on her forehead.

"Ah, yes, I believe I do," he mused. "I really do. Such a beautiful creature, the unicorn named Shadow. Have you seen him? He's here, you know, now that we are friends." Before she could snatch them away, he seized Arica's hands. "My dear niece, we two are alike, you know. Why fight it? Only you and I know what a fairy and a unicorn can do together! Never before — never! — have I felt such power!"

Sick with disgust, Arica wrenched her hands from his. She wiped them on her jeans, and Raden laughed.

Then his voice grew soft, coaxing. "Dear Arica, I want the same thing your grandmother wants: the union of North and South Bundelag. And my way of getting it is so much more peaceful. Let the South have its metals, its wood — what are they to us? Let them make their machines and scoff at our magic. They have no idea of the real power that is in this land. Only say the word, Arica, and the unicorns will be freed. With them as our servants, our power will be so great not even your world will be able to withstand us!"

Arica stood up. "You don't know the meaning of free. If you did, you would know that a unicorn is no one's servant," she said. "And I am not your 'dear' niece. I am your greatest enemy."

Even as she braved it out with her uncle, the voice in her mind was so strong she could hardly speak the words. Shadow's rage, his hatred, pounded in her brain like fists on drums. And yet there had been that moment — a terribly fleeting moment — when she had thought she could break through all that hate, to the creature underneath who was so desperate for help. If she could only meet Shadow, and speak with him again. She had to try, at least. She turned to the door.

Raden simply sneered at her. "Go to him, then. When you return, we will talk some more."

The trolls at the gate let her through without question. Up the pathway to the mountain she walked, to the wound in the rock she had made with the magic given to her by the unicorns, a place where she had hoped she would never be again.

Shadow stood silently, a sliver of grey against the blackness of Mine Mountain, a ghostly silhouette. Please, she thought, listen to me. We don't have to be enemies. I am nothing like Raden . . . Her hand shook as she reached up to run her fingers over Shadow's brow, his jaw, and across his silken nose. She brushed the hair away from his eyes, plucked a burr and smoothed his windblown mane.

True One, he said, *I am your enemy.*

"No," she whispered. "He is. Never you."

I shared my power with him. We travelled to Unicorn Valley and froze the unicorns in stone. The spell we cast together was very strong.

"I saw your work," she said. "And then you attacked me."

You would have tried to stop us.

"Yes," she said. "I would." She reached a hand toward him again. "I dreamed of you. So many nights I felt the burning of your anger."

My own kind did not want me, he said. *They drove me out.*

"Did you try to get back in?" she asked. "Did you even try to make peace with the others?"

The fairy is my only friend. He saved my life.

She shook her head. "He saved you so he could use you."

Shadow snorted and threw back his head in rage. Overhead, the silver of two distant moons reflected in his eyes like sparks off steel.

Arica stood back, breathing deeply, her heart

twisting within her. "There is much love in Bundelag," she said.

It is too late for love.

When she looked next, he was gone.

Back at the shed, Arica saw that Nue was already asleep. She stepped quietly, so as not to wake him, but paused just inside the doorway, her heart aching with a need for the warm and comforting touch of a friend. She would go to Wish, the best friend she had in all the world, in all of both worlds. She tiptoed back outside and moved over to where Wish lay, curled up in the hay. Arica knelt and pressed her shiver-wracked body against the unicorn's side.

But where there should have been warmth and scent of skin, there was only an icy slickness. Where there should have been flesh and living breath, there was now only stone, still and cold as death.

Arica placed her head upon the marble mane and clung, lost and hope-empty, in grief beyond bearing. Her tears splashed down across Wish's chiselled neck to drip into the straw beneath her knees. They sparkled like jewels in the moonlight as they fell.

There was now only stone, still and cold as death.

Chapter 10

Arica woke Nue just before dawn.

"We have to find the elves," she said as he blinked at her with bleary eyes. "Come with me."

Nue rose without argument. She waited outside while he dressed. At last he appeared, looking lumpier than usual.

Nue's face whitened when he saw Wish lying in the hay, silent and unmoving within her skin of stone. He walked stiffly beside Arica, his mouth hard and set, his eyes gazing at nothing. She offered no reason for what she was doing, and he asked for none. He had just seen all the reason he needed.

Arica had no trouble finding the elves. The only

building large enough to contain them all was the one she had lived in with them once before. This time, no troll guards stood at the door and no ropes bound them in long lines to each other.

The elves lay on their bunks in the silence of exhaustion. She wondered what had brought them back to this mine, and what kept them at this gruelling labour, day after day. Whatever the hold was that her uncle had over them, she *had* to break it. Surely they knew he couldn't be trusted to make good on any promise that he had made. If only she could convince the elves of that. It wasn't likely, but she had to try.

As she and Nue crept along the rows of cots, Arica noticed with surprise that over half of the beds were empty. This was a much smaller group of elves than the one who had been here before.

In the end, Nue was the one who found the leader of the elves. Arica had just about decided the quickest way might be to rouse the whole room. Then she heard Nue whisper her name. She heard a *thump* in the semi-darkness, followed by a strangled yelp. She arrived to find a fierce-eyed, sour-faced elf awake on his bunk. Nue had a dagger pressed against his throat.

"Sir," she said, trying to sound like her heart wasn't somersaulting into her throat. "We need your help."

"This is Bearlap," Nue growled through his teeth

to Arica. "I know him — I'm ashamed to say. Such a fine and noble example of elfhood. He tells lies as often as he can get away with it, and steals when he must, which is nearly all the time." The dagger pressed harder against his skin.

Bearlap flinched, and shook his head as best he could with a knife at his jugular.

"You're crazy, both of you!" he snarled. "Why would I help you when I have the chance of a lifetime here? And my good fortune is all because of you, pretty girl!"

"Me?" Arica replied. "I don't see — "

"When you blew up the mine with your magic the last time you fought Raden, you uncovered the richest vein of gold ever found in Bundelag. My people and I do the work, and Raden gives us a generous share of the profits. We will be rich — and more powerful than you can imagine. No more plowing fields or raking hay or shovelling dung from smelly stalls. What do you have to offer, that I should help you?"

Arica swallowed something painful that swelled in her throat. The rumours had been true all along. "I can't promise anything but freedom if we win," she said.

"What good is freedom when there is nothing but dirt to dig and pigs to slop?"

"I can see you've already made up your mind," she

said to the elf. "I can't compete with a fairy who offers you the world."

"Smart girl," said a mocking voice from the doorway. Raden strode forward, his eyes as black and cold as polished stones. "It takes you a while, but you always catch on."

"Uncle," said Arica, turning to face him.

"Something will have to be done about this," he said, his voice as slick as ice. "I can't have my house guests sneaking about, threatening the lives of my workers." He grabbed Nue's dagger and slipped it into his own pocket.

"Leave Nue out of this," said Arica. "It wasn't his idea."

Raden sneered. "Nice try, but I find it necessary to get you both out of the way. Od!" he called. "Take them to the pit. Throw them in. Perhaps a few days of it will cool their enthusiasm."

Od stomped forward. He shoved Arica and Nue out the door before him, across the compound and through the grey morning drizzle to the pit. They landed heavily at the bottom, their faces to the dirt, then struggled into a sitting position, shoulder to shoulder, their backs against the cold clay wall. The trolls hadn't thought to cover the hole above their heads, so the drizzle, which had grown into something much more serious, pattered miserably down upon them.

"I'm sorry, Nue," she said, wiping mud and dead leaves from her face.

"There's no need to be sorry," he said. "I couldn't very well visit the mine and not take in all the sights, now could I?"

She giggled in spite of herself. "You're right, it just wouldn't be the same without a stay in the pit."

They sat for a while without speaking. After what seemed like hours the wind shifted, leaving a small area where the rain couldn't reach. They shifted over to the drier spot and huddled there together for so long Arica began to wonder if their bones might fuse in place, never to move again. Suddenly there was a flash, then a single clap of thunder broke right above their heads. With it came Grandfather.

He appeared in the crack of lightning just before the thunder. An instant later the lightning dissolved, but Grandfather remained. He drifted down gently, his eyes aflame, his hair a fray of spitting threads and flickering ends. He floated in the air half a metre above the ground, turning this way and that, looking for the perfect spot. When he was satisfied, he placed his finger over his lips and regarded them thoughtfully through half-closed eyelids.

"Is he dead or alive?" whispered Nue, staring at Grandfather in confusion.

"That's something I've never figured out," said

Arica under her breath. "And he won't tell."

"Grandfather," she said aloud, "I'd like you to meet my travelling companion, Nue." The old man nodded absently, still deep in thought.

"Well, Granddaughter," he said at last, "You've got yourself into another fine fix. But don't worry, you'll be out of here soon. The time is near."

Arica took one long breath, clenched her jaw in annoyance, and said, "The time is near for what, Grandfather?"

He ran four fat fingers through his hair. It hissed, sparked and settled a little closer to his head. "Not my favourite way to travel," he admitted. "It's fast, but furious. You were saying?"

"*What* time is near?" she repeated, trying to sound patient.

"You need the sword," he said, as if that explained everything.

"The sword," she said, her voice rising. "It's . . . it's back in the shed."

"Take the sword," Grandfather said, as if he hadn't heard her. He was starting to look somewhat pale around the edges, now. His voice sounded hollow and thin. "It is time."

Arica's patience frayed suddenly, like a plucked thread. "How can I take it when it isn't *here!*" she shouted, jumping to her feet.

"But it *is* here," said Grandfather, and with that he vanished.

"My, my," said Nue, "That was an unusual experience. You fairies are such odd folk. But he was right about the sword. I brought it along this morning — without asking you, I'm afraid. Your mind was on other things." After a moment of struggling, he pulled it out from beneath his clothes.

"I thought you looked a bit lumpy," she said. "What would I do without you?" Then, "Nue, we've got to get out of here. Do you have any ideas?"

He stood up beside her, braving the raindrops. "You could climb onto my back," he said. Maybe then you could reach the top."

She shook her head. "It wouldn't work. Two of each of us stacked four-high wouldn't reach the top of this pit."

They stood together in silence, thinking. Then, "I have it!" cried Nue.

"What is it?" she asked.

"My magic is small and not powerful," he said. "but it *is* of the earth. Good elf magic can light fires, grow crops — even, at times, bring sunshine and rain — "

"Nue," she said impatiently. "What are you getting at?"

"Do you see all those little roots poking out of the sides of the pit?"

"Of course I see them!"

"I can make them grow until they become big roots, strong enough to hold us. Then we can just climb out of here!"

"Well then!" she exclaimed, clapping him on the back. "What are you waiting for?"

The elf knelt upon the ground and closed his eyes, looking for all the world like someone saying a prayer. Then he raised his hands, palms out, fingers pointing to the sky. He remained that way for so long, Arica wondered if he had fallen into a trance, or worse yet, asleep.

Then the tiny roots began to grow.

When they got to the size of strings, Nue opened his eyes and grinned at her. When they got to the size of ropes, she grabbed him and gave him a hug. They joined hands and danced around the pit — something that took about three seconds.

The roots grew larger and longer. In minutes, things were starting to get a little too crowded.

"Make them stop now," said Arica. "We can't pull ourselves up when they're sprouting out of the walls like that."

Nue closed his eyes and said something under his breath. The vines continued to swell and unravel.

"Nue!" she cried. The pit was filling completely with a twisting, winding mass of roots that burst from the ground, looped over her feet and up around her knees. They sprang out of the walls to press against her back and chest, choking off air. They tumbled down from above, coiling around her neck and arms like hungry snakes. And Nue was buried in them even deeper than she was.

With the strength of panic, Arica raised her sword and swung. The dull blade sliced through the roots like a whip through air. And all the growing stopped.

For a moment, the only sound was Arica's panting. Then, "Well, better late than never," Nue said cheerfully, if rather breathlessly, from a place far under a mass of roots.

"You had nothing to do with that," said Arica crossly. "It was obviously the sword." She began to clear a path to him. With barely a touch of the sword, the roots melted apart.

"Interesting. It must be some sort of spell-breaker," said Nue, in his old know-it-all voice.

Arica shook her head. You'd never know he had just missed being strangled to death.

Within minutes, they scrambled from the pit. Across the compound they ran, darting from building to building. In the elves' lodge they found hunks of bread and some apples. They crouched behind a cot to eat them. Arica was shivering so hard by this time that Nue pulled a blanket from one of the bunks and draped it over her.

The dull blade sliced through the roots like a whip through air.

"You look tired," he told her.

"You don't look so great yourself," she said, grinning. His clothing hung like a sack, more tattered than ever. His hands were caked with dirt, and his face smeared with it. When had all of the clutter and grime stopped bothering her? she wondered. It had sort of snuck up on her — this affection she felt for Nue. She wasn't quite sure what to do with it. Later, after Wish and the other unicorns were alive and safe again, she'd think it all over. In the meantime, she had other things to worry about. She sighed, and closed her eyes for a moment.

The next thing Arica knew, she was waking to the sound of a hundred feet clumping over old boards.

Nue squatted beside her, his hand on her arm. "The elves must be returning from the mine."

"Grandfather was right," she said, pulling herself up. "The time has come." She folded the blanket and replaced it on the bunk.

"What are you doing?" demanded Nue. "Get down, or someone will find us!"

"The time for hiding is over," she said. "I have to find Shadow, now. When Grandmother said 'Stop him!' I thought she meant Raden. But Shadow is the one who must be stopped."

"But you have no chance against Shadow!" cried Nue. "He's too powerful!"

"That may be." Arica held her father's sword out and looked at it thoughtfully. "Maybe I do have nothing to fight with but a sword I don't know how to use, and my own fairy magic — if I have any. And even if I do win, maybe it's too late to save the unicorns." Again her thoughts drifted to Wish, frozen into stone. "But I *am* their True One. They called to me through the crack. They trusted me. Now it's time to do what I came for."

Chapter 11

At the door Arica stopped and looked back one more time. Nue smiled, and the breath caught in her throat. She walked away quickly, before she could change her mind.

Arica saw Raden just before he saw her. He stood, still as a spectre in his long, black coat. Dark clouds heaved in the sky above his head. Lightning spit, brightening the bones of his face, darkening the skull-like hollows. She stood before him, not speaking.

His eyes widened when he saw the sword, and he stepped forward, reaching for it. Arica pulled back, and his hand dropped. He laughed. "Do you think that will save you? You will be destroyed."

She turned away from him without speaking, toward the path that led up to Mine Mountain. She knew that Shadow would be at the top, waiting for her. As she climbed and drew closer, she could actually see him, a paler shade of grey than the clouds that whipped around him.

For the first time since she had received it, the sword seemed lighter in her hand. It seemed to pull her upwards and on, giving power to her legs and strength to her lungs. She could feel the magic of it tingle up her arm — fairy magic, forged with spell and song.

The way grew more and more difficult, but somehow, instead of becoming tired, her energy increased. She lost track of the time. Minutes or hours — they were all the same. At the end, all she knew was the jagged peak of Mine Mountain, and Shadow, stepping forth to meet her.

Arica pulled herself up over the final ledge and stood, facing the unicorn. A screaming wind sucked the breath from her mouth and sapped strength from the marrow of her bones. Gusts of dust and gravel shrieked past her face and tore at her clothes. The thunder seemed to come from all around her and beneath her feet. Lightning webbed across a shattered sky.

Shadow struck at her silently, without warning, just as he had that first time, in Unicorn Valley. She saw the sudden movement and the blood-red horn, plunging at her breast. The fairy sword met the horn in mid-air. The crack of power that followed lit the sky on fire. Petals of crimson blossomed, then swirled off into the wind. The unicorn drew back his head, then struck again.

Without the magic of her father's sword, Arica would not have survived the first blow. She knew that, now. She was a mouse squeaking at a mammoth's feet. She simply followed the sword. It knew exactly where to go and what to do. Still, after a time she realized she was holding the unicorn at bay, nothing more. Minutes dragged by like endless hours. Her arm and shoulder throbbed with something beyond pain. The thin mountain air burned in her lungs. Waves of dizziness swept through her brain.

Then Shadow paused and pulled back, his nostrils flaring, his front hooves flailing at empty air. Arica gripped the sword against herself and waited.

"It's not too late to stop this!" she told him. "Even now, it's not too late." In answer, a sudden blast nearly threw her to her knees.

I have made my choice, came the bitter voice inside her mind.

"Choices can be changed."

Then Shadow raised his horn, and drew power from the lightning and the storm. The power lit his horn into a blaze of silver-red, and sent sparks exploding from his hooves. When he came at her again, the sword was wrenched from her grasp. It skittered across the ground and landed, tip-down, wedged between two stones. She rolled wildly, avoiding blasts of power that struck like lashing whips around her head.

The rest happened in slow motion, as if she were caught in some terrible dream. Magic burst once again from the tip of Shadow's horn, magic strengthened by the storm and by his own raging hate. It was unlike the magic of the other unicorns. It didn't tingle in her veins, all clean and blue, or shape to do her bidding.

Shadow's magic spattered black and thick, in drifts that choked her life and breath like smoke. She watched it come toward her, closer, and there was nothing she could do.

The magic hit and sucked her dry, then threw the husk away. She felt her helpless body as it tumbled over cracks in jagged stone. The cliff's edge rushed to meet her. She skidded on her stomach, teetered one brief instant on the brink, then dropped face-first toward the rocks below.

Seconds later she slammed into a ledge jutting out from the cliff's face. Brutal as the landing was, it saved her life. A few minutes passed before she was actually sure she was still alive, and a few more before her battered muscles responded to her brain. By the time she got back the strength to sit, Shadow was standing at the cliff edge above her, looking down.

She knew he could blast away the ledge as easily as a child snuffs out a candle. What was preventing him?

"Shadow," she shouted up at him, "choose again! It *is* possible! Let me help you find your way back to Unicorn Valley!"

He didn't reply, but still, he didn't blast the ledge and send her falling to her death. His face disappeared. She crept along the rock face, searching for handholds. The ledge got narrower with each rise upwards, but by the time it had petered out altogether, she was near enough to the top to pull herself up.

The wind drove at her, less violently now, but with rain. It had pasted the unicorn's mane and tail to his body, ran in rivulets over his ribs, and dripped off the end of his nose.

In moments Arica was drenched. She stood and studied Shadow through the lashing rain, knowing the next blast from his horn would be the last, for she would never survive it. But worse, she would have failed Wish, and all the unicorns.

She wondered if Grandmother's battle had ended better. And Grandfather — where was he now, at her darkest hour? *Darkest hour* . . . Something moved in her memory. The ogres . . . the rhyme . . . She thrust her hand into her pocket and touched the ogre eye. She remembered the words spoken by Thilug's father: *With ogre sight, no need to fight. Remember its power for darkest hour.*

Well, she thought, I'd have to look pretty hard to find an hour any darker than this one. She pulled the ogre eye from her pocket and unwrapped it.

The eye was not ugly, smelly or shrivelled, as she had expected it might be. Instead, resting on her palm was a glowing, emerald-green jewel, smooth and clear as glass. It sparkled like starlight on water, nearly blinding her. It glowed like a rising sun, throwing out showers of green and gold that spun in dizzy circles above her head.

In the centre of the shower, the vision came.

Arica saw the spell Shadow had cast upon his own kind. She heard the unicorns cry in silent agony as their skins hardened into stone and their eyes went blind, and the world fell silent around them.

She saw the blast of magic that was about to come from Shadow's horn, the one that would take her life.

She saw Raden drive his mother, the Fairy Queen, out of North Bundelag, and let the greedy humans in.

She saw the elves flee into the mountains until none were left to make the flowers grow.

She saw the ogres go underground, never to be heard from again. She saw all the trolls become a race of slaves serving the new king, Raden.

She saw Raden sitting upon his throne while the cracks between the worlds broke open. She saw cities cover the land, from the south border to the ice fields

She saw the blast of magic that was about to come from Shadow's horn.

in the north, and from the western mountains to the Valley of the Unicorns. She saw skies of blue turn as grey as ash, and green fields change to dust.

The last thing she saw was Shadow, swimming out alone into the churning sea, fleeing from the horror he had brought upon the land.

Not only did Arica see the events — she heard them, smelled them, felt them in her body. This was the vision the ogre eye had projected: the future of Bundelag without unicorns and their magic; a future without the Fairy Queen to protect the land and everything in it from ruin and despair.

And Shadow saw it, too. She sensed something wrench in his heart.

Arica had not known a unicorn could howl, and with such torment. The sound of Shadow's grief outblasted the thunder and the rain, filled her mind with fire, and shook the very rocks beneath her feet. He reared, his hooves slashing through the sheets of rain like knives. As he flung back his head, the water flew from his mane like tears that sprayed across her cheeks and chin.

Then it was over, and he was gone. She stood for one moment longer, dazed and uncomprehending, then slumped in silence to the ground and knew no more.

Chapter 12

Arica guessed she might still be alive because she kept hearing things. First, there was the hollow moan of wind against the mountain. Then came the cawing of birds somewhere over her head. Later she heard the clatter of stones, as if pushed aside by some small animal. Then more wind.

After a while she heard voices. They seemed all mixed up inside her head, but after a time she was able to pick out two or three distinct sounds rising above the others.

The first voice belonged to her grandmother, the Fairy Queen of Bundelag. But Arica knew the Fairy Queen was fighting at the border, days away from here. I must be dreaming, then, she thought. She couldn't allow for the other, grimmer possibility.

"She's still alive, thank goodness," said her grand-mother's voice. *She?* Was it someone at the border fight Grandmother was talking about?

"Pull my son's sword out of those rocks," ordered Grandmother, "and bring it to me. Look at this! There are burn marks all over this mountain. It must have been quite a battle."

"It was that, good Queen," came Nue's voice. "It lit up the whole sky."

"Have the elves brought up any blankets?" asked Grandmother, suddenly sounding rushed and busi-nesslike. "Good. Bring them over here."

Arica felt something soft settle around her. Who were they talking about? Oh — *she* must be *me*, she realized, though rather fuzzily. And things faded out again for a while.

The next sound Arica became aware of was one she thought she'd never hear again. It was the chime of silver bells speaking in her mind.

True Arica, they said.

So she wasn't dreaming. She was dead, after all, and in some kind of Bundelag heaven. For where else could Wish be alive and speaking, and no longer the lump of frozen stone Arica had said good-bye to forever?

"Don't leave me, Wish," she tried to whisper, but she lacked the strength to speak.

I will stay, the unicorn assured her. Then with the words came the gentle magic of her horn.

It touched upon Arica's head and tingled over the rest of her, clean and warm. And as she felt it move across her body, driving out the aching and the cold, it left behind a soothing numbness more healing than a mother's balm.

When she woke a long time later, Nue was at her side. She looked up at him through the foggy bliss of sleep and said, "Where am I?"

He leaned close to her and whispered something about the compound and Raden's mine. She took a sudden breath and struggled to rise. He held her gently down with his hand.

"It's all right," he assured her, placing a bowl of soup in front of her. "Eat this. Fairy Queen's orders."

She eased back onto her pillow, still holding the soup, and eyed him suspiciously. "What happened?" she asked, much more awake now. "What did I miss?"

"When you left me with the elves," he explained, "I waited for a while. But then things started to happen all at once. There were terrible crashes coming from the mountain, so I ran outside.

"There was lots of lightning, and then a big flash of

red light. A little later the whole sky lit up with green. It took me a while to figure that one out, but then I remembered the ogre eye."

Arica nodded, remembering. It was all coming back to her now. She shivered, then focussed on the sound of Nue's voice in her ears and the feel of the soup bowl, hot against her palms.

"When the scream came, I nearly jumped out of my shoes," Nue went on. "I knew it wasn't you who had screamed — no human voice could ever sound like that. No human could cause walls to tremble and mountains to rumble and shake.

"Then I saw Shadow coming down the mountain. I have never seen a unicorn run like he did then. He galloped with the lightning and the wind. There was magic all around him, and hoofprints of fire where his feet touched down. When Shadow was gone, the thunder stopped and the rain subsided and Wish came bounding across the compound. The spell over her was broken."

"What about the elves?" Arica asked.

"They're gone — for now, at least," Nue said. "My guess is, Bearlap and his men have sneaked away somewhere, with all the gold they could carry. But who's to say their greed won't get the better of them again? For now, anyway, things are pretty calm."

Arica sighed, with joy and sadness all mixed together. "Shadow and I saw a terrible future in the ogre eye," she explained. "We saw that in the end, he would destroy North Bundelag, and all the magic would be lost."

"It must have been a frightening sight," said Nue. "Is that what sent him running?"

Arica nodded. Then, "When did Grandmother get here?" she asked.

"Shortly after Shadow tore down the mountain. When she arrived, she and Raden had a little talk. I don't know what they said, but they both looked like they could spit daggers. Raden stomped off, but only after the Queen was done with him. No one has seen him or his trolls since."

"Be glad for that," said Arica, leaning back against her pillows.

"There's more," Nue went on eagerly, clearly elated to be the one breaking such big news. "The Fairy Queen has banished Raden from North Bundelag."

Arica's half-closed eyes flew open. "How is that possible?" she demanded. "How will Grandmother keep him out?"

"I don't expect him to stay away for long," agreed Nue. "But for now, he's safely gone."

She must have dozed off for a while, for when she opened her eyes Grandmother was sitting where Nue had been. It seemed that there were lines around her grandmother's eyes that hadn't been there before. But her smile sparkled with happiness and hope.

The old woman took Arica's hand in hers and leaned over to kiss her cheek. She didn't speak, but the pride Arica saw on her face said more than words could tell.

"Grandmother," she said, "How did your own battle go? Did you keep the Southern army from coming into North Bundelag?"

Grandmother nodded. "They were much stronger than we were, with their cannons and their guns. And there were so many more of them! They drove us back and back. Then just as they were about to break through our lines, the ogres arrived and helped us to win the battle. We couldn't have done it without them."

"They are my friends," Arica said simply.

"Yes," said Grandmother. "It is beginning, now. In the days to come, with your help, all the creatures of North Bundelag will join together to fight for freedom. And when that happens, the fairies that are lost on Earth will begin to remember who they are, and where they came from."

She reached out and drew Arica close. Then, practical as ever, she said briskly, "But that's all in the future. For now, what you need the most is plenty of rest, lots of love, and — "

"Let me guess," Arica said. "Chicken soup."

Epilogue

"Did I wake you?" asked Arica's father, tiptoeing into her bedroom. Moonlight — from only one moon — splashed in through the open window, washing the lines and shadows from his face. The door squealed on its hinges behind him. When it came to oiling, nailing or gluing, Father's philosophy was that, sooner or later, things fell apart or fixed themselves.

"No," said Arica. "I was awake. What are you doing up?"

"I had a strange dream, and I couldn't get back to sleep," he said, perching on the edge of her bed.

"What was it?" she asked, twining her fingers with his.

"I love you too, Father," she replied.

"I dreamed I was on the way home from work," he said, "driving by the swimming pool like I do every day. Then I was *in* the pool, one of those children splashing and shouting in the water. Then I wasn't in the pool any longer. I was in a . . . "

"Yes?" prompted Arica, gently.

"I was in a moat, beside a castle." He laughed, embarrassed. "It was just like in a fairy tale. Huge, all white and gold, with windows up high and flowers growing in the front. I was with someone. He was pulling me up."

"It sounds wonderful," said Arica, holding her breath. "Was there any more?"

"Yes — and this is where it got *really* outrageous. I was in a throne room, kneeling before a king, and the hand holding mine was pulling me to my feet. I raised my eyes to see his face, and I knew him — though I couldn't tell you his name. He was a young man, dressed in a purple robe, with a sword in his right hand. As he placed it in my own, I felt a rush of power run through my veins like fire. And that's all."

He stopped, confused. "It feels more like a memory than a dream," he added. "But that's impossible, of course." He shook his head, then leaned over and kissed her on the cheek. "I'll let you sleep, now. Love you."

"I love you too, Father," she replied.

He stood and took a few steps, then paused with his hand on the doorknob. "It was such a *strange* dream," he said, closing the door behind him.

"Not strange at all," Arica whispered.